Published by: Cinnabar Moth Publishing LLC
Santa Fe, New Mexico

Cover Design by: Faye @ Constant Creates

ISBN-13: 978-1-953971-28-9
Library of Congress Control Number: 2022933067

Awaken

LAUREN WAGNER

Chapter One
Natalia

They groomed me as a child. They taught me how to look, how to listen, and even how to die. They prepared me to live entirely for others. Die for others. I am destined to be the queen of Estancia, to live in a noble house filled with my own personal court and guards sworn to protect me at all costs, right until the moment of my death. Even as they tear me from my bed in the dark of night, I must remember this is their purpose, just as much as it is mine.

"May I say goodbye to my father?" The confidence in my voice covers the fear trembling in my gut.

"No, milady. There is no time."

The guard throws a musty cloak over my soft linen nightclothes. The stale smell overpowers the eucalyptus of the lotions on my skin, making my eyes water in disgust. I feel no better than a horse being led by the reigns.

I grip my golden slippers and run out of the house. My bare feet touch the wood of the floor and memorize the soft pitter-patter that vibrates in response. The same guard places me on top of the nearest horse. Black as midnight, silky as the hidden clothes under my cloak. My hands fumble for the reins as I lean forward and fight for my balance. I am not accustomed to riding horses.

I swallow hard and fight to hold back my tears. Queens do not cry. The overgrown trees cast a shadow over the wooden arch of my home, and the windows shine in the moonlight, but already I feel the memory of my home fading: the cayenne and paprika of the kitchen. The sun glittering off the windows in my rooms. I plead in my heart that father can hear my silent goodbyes.

I don't know how far we ride, but I know I have never been so far in my life. Branches tear at my face and snag on the wool of the cloak that protects my nightclothes from being ripped off my back. With my hair thrashing in my face, I steady my grip and close my eyes for a moment. A small movement, but one forcing me to take control of my breathing. In. Out. In. Out.

Three riders flank me. I know they are all mine, but in their silence, they seem like strangers. Years at my side and none have anything to say. They hold a mix of emotions in their eyes, sadness filled with a determination I know goes deeper than the blood pumping through their veins. This, too, is their purpose. Once I am gone, a new purpose will fill them with as much strength. I hope so at least. Father will need them.

We ride through parts of the kingdom unknown to me. The forest thins and the leaves become freckled with new shades of color reflecting off the light of the moon. But it's wrong. All of it is wrong. "This is not the way!" I yell over the wind, but my guards do not respond. I hold my tongue from yelling more and pull the cloak over my head, blocking out the view as much as I can.

My riders slow as the clouds cover over the light from the moon and we pull to a stop. Out of breath and chilled from the wind, I am pulled from the horse. "But this is not the way," I say once again. "This is not the place."

The oldest of the guards grips my arms gently. "Lady Natalia, we were asked to bring you here instead."

His touch holds a tender apology. He kneels so his face is even with my own. I feel like a child once more, being talked to as if I might shatter.

"But why?" My voice trembles over my confusion. "Tonight is the night. I should not be here."

He turns his head as his companions clear the brush at their side. He refuses to look at me, refuses to speak of their traitorous acts. Perhaps to even acknowledge what they are doing. What they have done.

"Please, milady. Do as we say and stay by the horses."

He leaves my side to help the other guards remove rocks from the bluff's anterior. The horse next to me trembles and snorts, pawing at the dirt with his front hooves. I pace with each rock set aside, even though I know better. Queens should not show fear. Should I run or trust in the men who have spent their lives protecting me?

They turn back to kneel in front of me, and my heart hardens. Their intentions are finally clear. "I am not to be sacrificed, am I?"

"No, milady, other arrangements have been made. You are to stay here."

"How long?"

"We cannot say."

Their fists clench and pull to their hearts as they silently apologize with a goodbye. Their eyes fill with tears as I nod at them, my understanding clear. This is where we must part. This is where I must stay.

Without a word, without question, I walk past them and step inside the grotto. Their heads drop as I pass. It seems as if they stay there frozen in time, statues molded into an aspect of regret. One by one they stand and turn towards me once more. My breath quickens as they replace the rocks at the entrance. One by one, their movements are played out in slow motion. I stand at the entry of the cave, refusing to step out of their sight. Even as the last of the rocks is placed over my view to the outside, I hold their gaze.

Goosebumps cover my skin as my eyes finally turn to search the hollowness of the cave.

A fire burns behind me. Nestled in a ring of stone, it rises up to meet the cracks on the cave's ceiling. My breath twists and turns with the flames, and my eyes water at the smoke. Gathering courage enough to sit near the heat, I turn my back on the small bed against the far side of the cave, across from the tinkling water pooling in the corner. My fingers trace the moisture off the walls to the trunk positioned next to the small cot. I open it with detachment, already knowing what lays inside. The trunk is filled with my personal trinkets and clothes. The necessities to pull me through the desolation.

This was not the plan. This is not what my future should hold.

Gathering my breath and clearing the dust from my throat, I stand and straighten the folds of my cloak. I inhale strength, pull off the hood covering my face, and slide my hands through the silky curls of my hair. It is the best I can do to try and tame the wild coils. I close my eyes and breathe in and out. In. Out. In. Out.

Only then do I open them with a brand-new sense of determination. Only then do I turn. Only then do I have enough courage to face the dragon in my midst.

Rising seven feet off the ground, he peels his chest off the damp floor and lifts his head in acknowledgment. He places the weight of his massive core onto his front talons and his serpent-like belly snakes around the circumference of the cave; then he relaxes on the ground. His glance is patient and expectant. He does not snarl or even rustle his scales.

I stand upright and pull back my shoulders. My fists clench at my sides. I force my muscles to relax to hide my fear. I remind myself how important it is a queen never show an ounce of distress, never show emotions. I force my breathing to slow and focus on the rise and fall of my chest.

Yet, here I stand, my fear laid like a blanket in front of a monstrous beast. "How long?" I say. "How long will I be kept here?"

His nostrils flare at me in question. He may play coy with me, but I know he understands.

"They will not stop until they find me. I am not to be forgotten." My courage to speak wavers, yet I tighten my heart in determination. I ask the questions that he has no answers for. Patient at first. Over and over, I ask my questions with polite resolve. "Who came to you?"

He watches in silence, his frame never inching any closer to my own.

"Why?" I say. "What will become of my people?"

Hours pass and my manners begin to weaken. My muscles grow weak and my back heavy from my stubborn stance. I feel my shell cracking with my impatience. My voice turns to pleads and screams. "Tell me! Tell me what happened! Tell me why!"

After what feels like hours, I drop to my knees and cry into my hands. I let the tears fall, as if it were the only other option. I let the stones under my knees dig into my clothes and the dirt from the floor stain the linen on my rear. I feel a hole in my chest open, and my disappointment floods out. This is not how today was supposed to unfold. This was not the future my father warned me of.

It is only then that the dragon pulls at the double coat of armor nestled on his skin. He relinquishes a shimmering blue scale from directly above his heart and uses his tail to push the treasure closer to me, silently urging me to take its contents.

"You want me to eat it?"

My eyes become heavy as I begin to understand, and all my hope hits the floor at my feet. I sniffle away my tears. I remove my cloak and sit on it like a rug. It scratches under my weight, and pricks at my skin. I can focus on this, I tell myself. All of my life, I have done what I was told. Today should be no different. I reach out to grasp the piece of his flesh. My hand trembles and lingers above the scale.

I look at him, pleading for a different option.

He gestures toward his mouth, and I imitate his actions. Slow but determined, even a little resolved. My fingers find their way to my lips as I allow them to part. The scale dissolves in my mouth, tasting of ash and that of my unobtained future. I let the remnants slide down my throat and refuse to gag up the contents. My nerves tingle and a numbness flows through my limbs. I feel my eyes flutter and my mind slow. The rhythmic pulse of my heart steadies with that of the dragon and the magic takes effect.

Chapter Two
Natalia

I know I wake more often than I should. I feel it in his mannerisms, the way he looks at me each time I open my eyes. The way his head tilts to the side, as if he is trying to shield his annoyance.

It is vile each time I wake. Nausea cramps at my insides, and my fists rub at the sleep in my eyes. I scream at the dizziness that pulls at me. I scream as I attempt to hinder my trembling limbs. The dragon watches my every move. Patient frustration lingers in his gaze, yet he never makes a sound. He never offers companionship or any sort of emotion at all. Sore from the stone beneath me, anger at my dragon keeper mounts. But my grief is never comforted and eventually my tears subside.

Time passes and after nearly a dozen dragon scales and dreamless states, I make my way to the pool of water still bubbling at the dragon's tail. The water's flow offers a clear sign of survival. But I never wanted survival. I wanted something so different it aches in my bones. I wash and clean my body as well as my soul, grateful that my Keeper turns his head to offer me privacy. I strip off my ragged nightgown. I wash it and change into another from the trunk.

I try to converse with the dragon, but talking to him is futile, and I retreat to the comforts of the small bed. Another scale is offered, and in defeat I accept another slumber.

The sleep given to me is not restful or filled with dreams. It is hard. It is rigid and temperamental, knocking me into a place far from consciousness. A place lost between sleep and alertness. I am solid, firm, like a bear hibernating in the winter.

Countless dreamless sleeps and failed conversations take their toll. I am no longer fully here. Not real enough to be a ghost, but too unfortunate to perish.

"Kill me," I beg. "Use that fire-blazing breath and kill me."

I exert the little energy remaining in my soul and flank him. "I've suffered. I have agonized, ached, and grieved. Your torture has reached its course. Please. Please, Keeper, please. Kill me." I can't do this anymore. I can't hide like a prisoner knowing all I know. Day after day of waiting is more torturous than death itself. What would have been? What should have been? What will become of me now?

A small turn of the head offers his denial.

I lunge at him, using every last breath to hit and kick the serpent who hides me from the world. Never once does he wince away from my pathetic wrath. Never once does he attempt to soothe my pain.

I slide my body down his side, slump my shoulders and cover my face with my trembling hands. "I was supposed to be proud of my death," I whisper. "It was supposed to mean something." How was this supposed to be better? How would death alone in a cave be preferred over a predestined course of sacrifice?

My eyes stare into the shadows and I make up memories in my mind. I am playing with my mother in a field, wrestling in the grass with siblings. I am climbing trees with other children from the village, picking fruits for festivals filled with singing and dancing. But then the shadows fall, and I realize I am alone once more. There is no mother to play with me. No siblings to teach me bad behaviors. I am alone now more than ever. I imagine a goodbye with my father. His eyes fill with pride as he watches me leave. I imagine my wedding day, a crowd cheering at my feet. And once more the shadows fall to darkness.

I refuse any more water or scales of his flesh. My body screams for nourishment, yet I continue to refuse. I want a say in how it happens. I want him to know I am angry and when this is all said and done feel regret about his choices. I want him to know it was not supposed to happen this way.

I stare at the small glimmer of light fading into the darkness of my cave. It sneaks in through the cracks thirty feet above my head and disappears into the walls high above my reach. I imagine the light as my only hope, but it lingers too far from my grasp.

I lose count after a few days. My vision blurs and my muscle aches become too strong to ignore. I feel his tail lift me to the small, unfriendly cot, and I feel the ground-up scales placed on my chapped lips. The ashy flavor is now a distant memory and the salty powder dissolves into bursts of flavor: cinnamon and honey, cocoa and mint. I close out the lingering light from the ceiling and the fading embers from the fire. Darkness prevails, and I finally find refuge in an endless sleep.

Chapter Three
Quinn

His anger with his father drives the pickax. It grinds into the ancient stone and shatters it. "I should be in school," he murmurs. "Pissed off that I'm stuck in school rather than on some lavish field trip across the wastes of the world."

Chipping away at the stone, he ignores the protocols his father has laid out and smashes at everything in his sight. Years and years of warnings, and his movements are still careless. "Archeological dream site, my ass." He shouts over the hammering racket of the two grad students behind him. "Algebra! I should be bitching about algebra instead of this God damn physical labor!"

Their laughs travel across the field but remain fruitless.

He kneels, brushes the sweat off his brow, and moans up at the sky. Frustration eats away at his will. "There has got to be some sort of child labor law that is against this sort of shit." Rolling to the balls of his feet, he readjusts his stance for more stability and, in the heat of the sun, tries to ignore his muscle aches. The humidity weighs heavily on his skin. His skin rests thick with perspiration.

His final swing shatters the unforgiving ground. The earth cracks and quakes under his feet. Hollowness appears beneath him, and he falls through the earth. He screams and grasps for a handhold as he plummets into the darkness. His left hip hits the hard rock on the ground, followed by what he thinks must be his head. For when he opens his eyes and takes in his surroundings, he knows what he sees can't be real. He knows the girl sleeping on the cot in front of him can't be real. He knows the blanket covering her, the rose-colored flush on her cheeks, and the brilliant brunette locks lying underneath her head, cannot be real. His staggered steps over to her must be as fictional as the slow rise and fall of her chest.

She is a gorgeous concoction of his mind set up like some sort of trap. He stares at the sick, twisted joke the universe is playing on him with sleep caressing her eyes. He always thought treasure would shine like gold but here and now, his thoughts fight him. He reexamines his reluctance to take part in his father's expedition.

He bends to a mere inch from her face and feels her breath touch his mouth. Wishing that her lips would wake and find their way to his own, his fingers run down the side of her cheek. Warmth from her skin engulfs him. He closes his eyes and takes another breath. "This is a dream," he whispers.

He ignores the sounds above him. He ignores the shouting and the stomping of feet echoing from above. All he focuses on is the girl. The girl sleeping in front of him who couldn't possibly be real.

"Quinn! Quinn!"

Ryan and Darius, his father's favored grad students, call to him. Dirt from the ceiling drifts to his head from the rumble of their feet, yet his mouth lingers close to the girl, wishing for a taste of this fantasy his heart has dreamed up.

His heart stops as the girl lying in front of him whimpers. Her arms reach above her head, and her toes stretch out beyond her coarse woolen blanket. She turns over on her side, and he stumbles back, tripping over the stones and boulders that fill the space behind him. He rubs at his eyes and feels for a bump on his head. Nothing.

Darius plummets to his side with a rope pulled taut around his waist. "Quinn! Quinn, are you hurt?"

After a quick inspection of Quinn, his eyes find the girl, and he, too, stares. Taking a deep breath, Darius finally speaks the words that cry true to Quinn's find, "Holy shit."

Chapter Four
Natalia

I wake to a set of ocean blue eyes filled with disbelief and a smooth, unyielding face. Shock holds his cheeks tight. His lips purse together.

I am dreaming, I tell myself. One more moment and the dreams will subside. I will take another scale and my dreams will diminish. But until then, I remain in a daze. Confused with magic or maybe poisoned with despair, I feel my body move, but only in acute awareness. My muscles scream at me as my toes curl and my fingers stretch. I have a vague memory of moving my head from side to side. My eyes search for the Keeper, in fear he might stop this intrusion, yet I find only stone in a glorious lizard shape that reaches to the far end of the cave. He, as well as his magic, has gone.

The blue eyes belong to a man. Not yet filled to his height, but no longer built like a boy. Strange clothing falls too loose on his frame. His dirty shirt tucks into ripped pants held by a worn leather belt. Grime covers his pale skin. His hair is short and rumpled at the top of his head.

A man drops from the sky next to him and speaks a language not of my own. I listen for my breath. In or out. But in my shocked silence, I feel my heartbeat.

"How did you find me?" I say softly. My unused voice is hoarse and shaky. Tears roll down my face as the realization hits me. My back is sore. My head is heavy. My stomach is filled with knots: this is not a dream.

Both men stare at me with wide eyes. Several silent moments pass before Blue Eyes takes a small step closer, his eyes reaching their own conclusions.

He speaks in a language unknown to me, but the softness in his tone is comforting. His fingers are unsteady as he reaches his hand out, urging me to take it. Unfolding from my cot, I let my blanket fall to the ground. I stand, though my limbs tremble at the memory of how to hold my own weight. I lean back toward the cot to brace myself as I fall to my knees on the hard stone floor.

The men continue to stare at me, their eyes heavy with concern and disbelief. The older one begins to shout commands toward the sky, screaming at the hole letting the darkness escape. Blue eyes stands firm, his gaze never once moving from my face. His arm remains outreached.

His eyes are bluer than any I've ever seen, not in my time outside the cave and never once in my dreamless sleeps. The light from above falls on his head like a message from the stars, and his eyes twinkle like fire. He looks at me, *like* me. Not like his queen or his sacrifice. Just me.

Ropes and mechanisms heavy with silver are sent tumbling down as more men continue to shout at each other. Yet, the world remains still.

The blue-eyed one steps to the side to take hold of one of the ropes and approaches me with apprehension in his gait. His arms reach out, and he silently asks permission to tie the rope around my waist. I don't move as he kneels. I am frozen in place, held in a moment of hope that seems forbidden. Nodding his head at me, half of his mouth moves into a smile, leaving the other half anxious. He waits still, stolen in a place in time, until the slight nod of my head gives consent. His hands brush against my torso, sending tingles up my spine. The hole in my chest begins to fill at the feel of someone's touch on my skin. He wraps his fingers around my own and folds my fingers around the rope.

He helps me to a stand and pulls the rope taut. My heart begins to race at the intent of the line, how he plans to save me from the depths of the earth and pull me into the sky. "No." My voice trembles. "No." This is wrong. All of it is wrong.

He speaks more words to me that I struggle to understand.

"No," I say louder. I stand straighter and begin to back away, back to my cot and my devilish refuge. I did not wake just to find death once more.

He pauses and motions to the man handling the ropes. Their conversation is short, urgent. He looks at the man behind him. Not arguing the change of plans. The other man slowly begins his retreat to the sky, still shouting demands to the top of the hole.

I stare in silence. Confused. Unsure. Absolutely prettified.

Blue eyes motions between us. He holds his arms out and beckons for me to come near him, silently pleading for me to trust him. Fear ripples through my veins as I try to remember my courage. He moves his body closer to mine, his muscles tensing as he reaches for the ropes and metal devices he clicks in place on his clothes. He wraps one arm around me, and I feel myself turn feverish at his touch. He grabs the rope above his head with his free arm and lifts my weight into him with the other.

Feeling sinful with my chest so close to his, I can't help but hope I am making the right choice. Does his heart beat as fast as mine? My breath quickens as we rise to the balls of our feet and my eyes clamp shut. With shaky palms, I place my arms around him. I squeeze tight as we begin the ascent.

Although his strong hold around my waist gives me comfort, our feet rise further and further from the ground. Heat rushes from his chest to my own, while his breath whispers at the nape of my neck.

I do not look back at my lonely dungeon. I don't look once more for my Keeper or anticipate scales placed on my tongue. Grunts and shouts come from above, but his blue eyes remain calm, steady. With each blink of his gaze, my chest tightens, urging me to feel more than just fear.

When the light hits me, the truth of my escape hits me so hard I feel my heart stop. The hope of it left so long ago I fear I am not ready. What is it I will find? Already I miss the refuge of darkness. The safety in its silence. The light burns my skin like fire, racing over my limbs, and climbs to the sockets of my eyes. I bury my face into the folds of his neck and whimper with the pain of the light. The agony increases and no longer can I hold on. I drop my arm from the sturdy grasp holding me and pull it over my head to shield my eyes from the torture of the light.

The rope drops at the sudden shift of weight. He drops his other arm to hold me tighter, and we begin to swing. Back and forth toward the hardness of the walls, and the cave closes in on me once more. The gravity of it pulls at my toes. It dances with the remnants of my hope forcing dizziness upon me.

He soothes me as we swing, suspended in the air like flies. While the grunts and shouts persist above, he whispers into my ear. He undoubtedly feels the quick succession and pained rise and fall of my chest. I tell myself I can focus on this. Ignore everything else and focus on the movements of the man with blue eyes. He whispers until I find the strength to pull my arms away from my head and grab hold of his neck once more. Even through the pain, I know I need him. I need him to get me out of the darkness. I need him to be my light.

The swinging rope slows and our ascent begins once more. His free hand caresses the back of my head as he hums comforts into my ear. My breath begins to steady as I concentrate on the timbre of his voice. He is here to save me. He is here to make everything right once more. I focus on my breath and remind myself to breathe in and out. In. Out. In. Out.

The groaning and grunting above the rope grow louder as we climb to the sky. As the light completely surrounds me and my sides scratch against the stone dirt of the ground, his grasp on me begins to loosen. Several arms reach for us at the surface, and I spill onto the ground that now offers my freedom.

Chapter Five
Quinn

Her whimpers become painful to hear as the full wrath of the sun falls on her face. In daylight, he is dumbstruck at her beauty. Elegant brown curls fall on her face and shimmer off the olive skin under the soft, white gown that reveals her curves. Not only are her curves exposed but also her cowering fear. He lies next to her on the ground, his breath just as ragged and short as hers. "Blanket!" he shouts to those who helped pull her out of the darkness. "Get a damn cover for her!" The minutes feel like hours as he becomes her cover.

His father arrives first, a picture of calm and understanding. "Pick her up. Gently. Crouch as low as you can and move to the tents. We will keep you both covered."

The strength of his father's palm on his back soothes him. "Do you think she will allow it?" He lifts her off the ground and cradles her like an infant in his arms. She does not resist as she covers her face with both her forearms. His feet stumble as he sprints to save her from the sun.

Her whimpers seem to shorten yet feel deeper with the tears she is holding back. The crew stumbles around him, maintaining the cover his father promises. They reach the tent just as her whimpers turn into screams. He lies her on his cot and hurries to fetch his shades and a ball cap to cover her face. His father rushes to zip the tent flap, shielding them from the midafternoon light.

The small tent feels very crowded as the four men kneel down in front of her. It's absurd, utterly absurd. How it happened he cannot begin to understand. Pulling her legs up to her chest, she wraps her arms around her pale legs. Her toes peek out from under her silk nightgown. Hair curls around her face, the cap shielding everything but the soft arch of her chin. Her skin is blistering from the sun.

"What's your name?" his father says, his tone determined yet kind.

Her eyes turn up to him, lost under the hat and sunglasses too large for her face.

"Tell us your name."

She lets out a whimpered cry as her eyes plead to him. "Shneex an a newy huy do yea."

"That's not Spanish. Not Italian." He runs his hand over his face. "Does anyone have any idea what language that is?"

"It's not English," Quinn mumbles.

His father's eyes flash to him, silently cursing his sarcasm.

"En guen, me nosa, berrios els nasa," she whispers.

He pats his chest. "Quinn." He taps his father's chest. "Bailey. Darius. Ryan." He points to each man.

She looks into the eyes of each man as she thinks it through. He repeats the process once more. She taps her chest. "Natalia."

They smile at her, relishing in the role of her r's.

"Quinn," he says again. "Seventeen." As quickly as he can, he draws seventeen tally marks in the dirt at their feet. "Ryan, twenty-three." Drawing six more tallies, he points to Ryan. "Darius, twenty-five." Drawing two more, he points again. "Bailey." He thumbs his father. "Old." His father huffs in response, but keeps his mouth shut.

She erases nine tallies from the dirt and pats at her own chest.

"Sixteen," Quinn murmurs. "You are sixteen."

His father runs his hand through the thickness of his hair. "I need to call this in. Figure out who she is and get her back to where she came from. Ryan, get her some water and food. Darius, head back to the Jeep and get the satellite up. Quinn, stay here with her. Keep up what you're doing. Do whatever you can to find out whatever the hell got her out here so many days from civilization." Patting Quinn's shoulder, Bailey and his grad students leave them alone in the tent.

"Hey, Dad!" he shouts at the last minute.

"Yeah?"

"I'm sorry, this is way better than Algebra."

"Not for her, Quinn. I very much doubt that it is for her."

Chapter Six
Natalia

With my skin boiling and my breath ragged, my eyes plead to close and return to my slumber, perhaps to take comfort in the cot behind me in the safety of Quinn's nearness. Maybe sleep will offer me a sense of sanity, perhaps even understanding.

I have been saved, pulled from a darkness so deep it shattered my future. My savior sits in front of me, the concern on his face vibrating across each of his movements. He has only known me for only a matter of hours, yet already I know he cares. There is no judgment in his eyes.

I should not feel so wronged. But I don't know this stranger. I feel too exposed and I worry about my instant desire to trust him. The burning on my skin does not feel like a dream, nor does the exhaustion pulling on my weight. But yet, I can't help but question my new reality. Dizziness consumes me as he continues to converse, and eventually I stop trying to understand him. Not out of desire, but out of weakness. All of my strength has abandoned me. Instead, I find comfort in his company, a human rather than a serpent, a man speaking to the secret confines of my heart.

He stops asking his questions. Whatever he wishes I were to know is left unspoken. I succumb to the will of my weary bones and lie down on my side. With my gaze focused on the blueness of Quinn's eyes, the last of my tears fall. I fear he will be gone if I sleep, that his crooked smile will disappear into a dream I am too soon to forget.

I plead with my heart to wake once more. I close my eyes, and for the first time since forever, I sleep without magic.

Chapter Seven
Quinn

The sun begins to set before the three men finish their chores.

Natalia wakes from several hours of sleep to drink the water offered to her, though she eyes it suspiciously. The crackers she does not touch.

Quinn admits defeat after failing to get any more information out of her.

"Three days," Bailey says. "The nearest trading post says it will take at least three days to get officials out here." He places his hands on his hips as he searches the horizon. "They are going to check the nearest towns and local tribes, but from their database there has been no report of a missing girl matching her description." His eyes fix on Natalia, sitting in the shaded tent. "They are going to bring a linguistics professor with them. Try and help as much as they can."

"That's a start," Quinn says.

Bailey scratches his head. "How is it possible? We have been scouring this area for weeks with no sign of how she got into that cave. How the hell is it possible? There must be a way inside, underground."

Quinn shrugs.

Wiping his hands over his eyes, Bailey's brows straighten. "Let's get her fed tonight. Quinn, you can stay with me for the next few days and give her your tent as her own. Tomorrow we'll go back into the cave with proper lighting and pullies." He paces in the direction of the hole. "It's been recent. I'm sure of it. She would have smelled far worse if not."

They coax Natalia out of the tent with reassurances that the sun is setting. They leave the hat and sunglasses on and a blanket wrapped over her small frame. Starting a fire and cooking a meal, they all resume their nightly tasks, quietly, unsure of their next move, unsure of what to expect. They strip feathers off a bird Darius captured for the night's supper and move tarps around the tent to reorganize the campsite's kitchen. Although it keeps the humidity in and the breeze out, the tarps provide shelter for Natalia away from the lingering sun.

Quinn breathes in her smell of eucalyptus, an intoxicating perfume that keeps him up at night. His father is right about the timeline. If she was down there for a while, she wouldn't smell so good. But the light. It's the light that contradicts his prediction. The light had such a horrid effect on her.

She stays quiet at dinner, and once offered a plate, finds a seat next to Quinn. The men gulp down their food, but she eats her meal like a lady at a banquet with petite bites and elegant sips. Either she detests the food given to her, or she is not nearly as hungry as Quinn believed she should be.

Silence persists at the table through the entirety of the meal, with none of the typical banter between the four men. None of them marvel at the day's finds or complain about the climate. Silence consumes them.

They clean up from dinner, then sit at the fire. She follows suit, and no one dare say otherwise. She pulls off the sunglasses and examines them. The hat remains on her brown locks, and the blanket nestles around her shoulders.

"Quinn. Bailey. Darius. Ryan." She squints and stares up at the now sparkling sky. "I eh guen." She nods her head at them and closes her humble eyes in the process.

"You're welcome," Quinn whispers.

Chapter Eight
Natalia

They want me to sleep in the tent overnight, but the tent is just a smaller version of the cave. I am not ready to be confined once more to darkness. I am not ready to be left alone. I choose a bedroll and a soft pillow to lie my head instead. Resting under the stars, I will never choose anything else. The others pace at the foot of their own separate sleeping quarters and worry about allowing me to sleep outside by myself. My guards would have done the same.

Quinn places his sleeping roll near mine, then one by one the others follow suit. The crackling of the fire dies to ashes and my rescuers fall one by one into the sleep I fear more than life itself. I cannot recollect the landscape around me with the dirt spread between patches of lush grass and towering boulders. The whispering line of trees that lie only a few miles away are the only familiar signs I see. Touching my face, I recall the thick forest and the branches scratching my limbs as I was rushed into the cave. I remember the stampede of my horse jumping over the stumps that remain somewhere within that forest. I glance back at the cave and wait for the dragon that never emerges.

The forest and the hole I was pulled from are the only signs of reality that make sense. That and the stars. Oh, gods, the stars.

Moving my gaze from the foliage, I find Tempras, the seven stars of life showing me the path toward the true God of light. I follow his light back towards the line of the forest as I imagine my father running through the thicket. I imagine him embracing me in his arms and taking me home.

I do not sleep.

The men begin to stir around me well after the darkness puts them to sleep. How odd their mannerisms. Their clothes hang too loose with too many colors, and they do not carry shields or flags to hold their insignias; thus their origin remains foreign to me. Hollow furniture, drinking water from bottles, even the slant of their native tongue is strange.

The fire marks the center of their tiny camp, but the tents are enough for a dozen men. Tables and tools line up beneath them. Stones rest in silver bowls and pictures and maps cover every flat surface. It is only their four sleeping tents that I find familiar, though the material remains odd. It is too smooth to the touch and remains too quiet in the wind.

As the sun begins to emerge, I find delight that I can bear its rays without the dark mask covering my face. There is nothing more beautiful than the orange and purple folding over the horizon. My silence turns into a whispered song.

Sunrise come, dark be gone
Life and water. Fruit and stone.
Born again, save my king,
Take my breath, hear me sing.

Placed in darkness, left to sing
Rejoice in loss, rejoice and sing.
'Til the dragon, her bounty sold,

He took it all, fire and life,
Her heart lay pierced without the knife.

Be here not made, be here strong.
Grow from the ground, above it all.
You shall not falter; you shall not wither.
Shell of the winter, summer, and fall.
Be here not made, be here strong.

You will grow, you will stand.
Dragon breath, fire and ice.
Roots of gilt, fruits of silver.
Be here not made, be here strong.

My eyes turn from the sky and look into Quinn's tender gaze.
I fear I have woken him and my insides leap. His hair sweeps over
his forehead, rumpled from a restless sleep.

It was not his singing that woke him. Not the rising of the sun
nor the heat rising with the day. It was his heart. He whispers to
me, touches his eyes, and silently pleads.

I instantly obey and fall asleep safe in his watch.

Chapter Nine
Quinn

Hours later they sit together at the hump of the plain, watching as Darius, Ryan, and Bailey hop into the depths of the earth.

Quinn is torn. He longs to enter the cave with his father. It is a lifetime opportunity, but he can't leave her alone, not knowing what she faced in the cave. That and there is something about her that quietly panics when he wanders away. Her eyes follow him where ever he goes. She only falls asleep when she knows he is watching over her.

They sit for what seems like hours, she with her arms wrapped around her knees, never once taking her eyes off that damn hole. Her face, still hiding underneath his baseball cap, cowers.

When the archeologists finally emerge from the ground, their faces are unreadable. Bailey joins them while Ryan and Darius huddle at the edge of the hole and pull something heavy to the surface.

With his eyes scrunched and his nose wrinkled, Bailey whispers in a croaking voice. "How?" He pauses and tilts his head. "Every wall is smooth. There's no way in, aside from the top. There is not one inch of rock disturbed." He strokes the length of his face, leaving striped smudges of dirt on his cheeks. His voice stumbles as he meets Natalia's gaze. "They are bringing up your stuff."

"Stuff?" Quinn says.

Natalia stands as Darius and Ryan pull the trunk over the side of the embankment. Clutching her hands together, she kneels once more as the two men set it in front of her. Her hand skims past the yellow-painted jaguar and blue-feathered serpent carved ornately on the side. She picks at the lock and pulls out necklaces and bangles of jade and obsidian, ornaments of feathers and weaved bracelet cuffs. She throws earspools carved in perfect symmetry to the side of the trunk and abandons the golden coins that fall to the dirt. She pulls at the soft green linen folded neatly on top of the chest and ignores the jewelry and trinkets. She sighs and heads to the stream for what could only be privacy.

They wait. All of them, staring at the hole just as she had moments before. They twiddle their fingers and pretend to look busy, kicking their feet in the dirt as they wait for her to return. They stare at the coins and pace in circles. Should they search through her possessions while she takes her time at the other side of their camp? If Quinn were to pick up the coins to analyze, would he lose her trust the moment she appeared and accused him of stealing from her? The gold reflects off the sun, but the artifacts remain in place. Even Bailey stares at the treasures with a hunger in his eyes but keeps his hands rigid at his side.

She appears, looking ravishing in a linen bodice that pushes up her breasts and leaves her hips slim. It falls off her shoulders with intent and purpose, the flowing skirt ending at her calves. Golden slippers protect her small feet. Her hair curls and flows down the length of her back but remains wet from its wash. The smell of eucalyptus is stronger than before.

Quinn can't take his eyes off her.

She holds the baseball cap in her hands.

Hearing his father clear his throat, he springs into action. He takes the cap from her and leads her to the small table in the makeshift outside kitchen, leaving the remainder of her artifacts behind. Motioning for her to sit, he places a notebook in front of her and sits at her side.

He places a pencil in her hand. "Tell us."

She looks at him, confusion in her eyes.

He takes the paper in his hands and draws a simple forest with four tents resting outside the line of timber. Motioning with his arms, he says, "This is our camp." He turns the page in the notebook and pushes it back to her.

She hesitates for a moment, her eyes on him. His reassurance and understanding seem to soothe her, and she begins to draw.

What she draws raises further questions. Not only at her skill, but at the story that unfolds. A castle rests on a hilltop. Moats flow out in each direction. The forest rests to the west of the castle, overgrown. She fills the emptiness of the page with ceiba and jicaro trees. Pointing at the trees drawn on the paper, she nods at the forest to the east. "Estancia," she says.

His father is standing nearby. "There is a myth of Estancia. No one I know has been lucky enough to excavate it. No one has been lucky enough to even find it." His hand finds his chin, and he scratches his goatee. "Myths say it was deserted. No cause or reason ever found. Like the Mayans and Aztecs who just picked up and left, or Atlantis, I guess. If she speaks the truth, I would drop everything here and head there now." He stares at the darkening forest. "It would be the dig of a lifetime."

"The Mayans and Aztecs were killed off. I think that is a little different than disappearing into thin air," Quinn says.

His father snorts. "Semantics."

"What if it's still there? What if that's where she came from and digging wouldn't even be necessary?"

"It's possible, I suppose. The canopy of the trees is capable of hiding nearly anything. God knows that after this anything might be possible." Bailey rubs his tired face. "Let's wait and see what happens with her first. Decide what needs to be done after that."

As they start to clean up the table, Quinn places her drawing in her hands. Their eyes meet. He imagines a city filled with people, all with brown curls, olive skin, and stark brown eyes. Lost in time, they all speak a language vanished from the world, and dress in linens so soft he could lose himself in the touch. In the middle of the city, he imagines Natalia's castle and a family missing her. Perhaps even searching for her. Probably. Almost certainly.

He can't help but wonder if it is archeology if people still practice a lifestyle resembling the treasures they dig. Maybe they wouldn't even need to dig. For all he knows they could be invited into Natalia's kitchen and rewarded for her return. "You found our missing girl? Please be rewarded with some treasure." He smirks at the thought. Even in his short time with her, he knows far too well that she is worth more than any treasure.

The next few days follow a similar pattern. Natalia stares at the darkened sky through the night and only closes her eyes to sleep once Quinn awakens to watch over her. During the day, she draws more pictures: horses running through the forest in complete darkness, dragons curling next to fires, and an abandoned bedroom with no sign of distress.

Argentinian officials arrive as promised on day three, sweating and unhurried in their drive up to the camp. The linguistics professor beside the two officials looks positively out of sorts. The officials stroll into the outdoor kitchen in uniforms and bandanas shielding sweat from their eyes. He, however, walks up in khaki shorts and flip flops, annoyance plastered all over his face.

The linguist seats himself at the table under the covered shade and looks at Natalia and the sun blisters slowly beginning to heal on her skin. "Let's talk."

She folds her hands into her lap in full anticipation of an attempted conversation. She steals glances at Quinn, and a worried frown mars her perfect forehead.

"Let me hear you speak, and let me figure out where you are from," the linguist says. He motions to his mouth and spreads his fingers apart in the process. His gesture is blatantly clear.

Her voice trembles as she speaks. "A hoy nei de box en Natalia. Ey me doungn en box. I eh guen."

Staring at her, his posture tightens as he leans toward her. "Again?" he says. She stares momentarily, then speaks once more. He wipes the sweat from his brow. "Tu en guen?" he says, his eyes growing wide. "En stus est? Tri new ghue?"

"Ayh. En stus est."

He is silent for several minutes. She is quiet as well, trained to pay close attention to the man who now understands her. The only man who understands her.

Quinn waits at her side, pulling at the straps on the tent's pullies. Bailey stands motionless at his side, fidget free.

"She speaks Anxcian," the linguist finally says. He circles his fingers around both of his temples. "A dialect dormant for a few hundred years."

"Keen wy es yoon?" Her voice rises as never before. Her eyes plead with the linguist.

He squints at her. "Kien hundos kien dos."

She jumps up from the chair and stumbles away from the unshaven man. The chair falls to the ground as her face pales, and her body begins to shake.

"Neh," she says. "Neh." She begins to cry and falls backwards, panic dripping from her face. Dropping her arms to the grass under her toes, she bends her head down, hiding it in her knees. Her fingers grasp the flesh of the ground and rip grass out of the dirt. Her cry becomes a scream.

None of them speak. None of the men even move. They watch in astonishment at her outrage. Quinn curses his hesitation. The girl is hysterical in the middle of nowhere, and not one man knows what the hell to do.

Panting, her screams turn back into cries. She pushes to her feet and races for the hole she was pulled out of.

They all follow, the linguist closest to her.

"Kien de dos beatyin!" she shouts into the depths of the earth. "Kein de dos beatyin!" She falls once more to her knees and continues to cry.

Quinn kneels in front of her. He lifts up her chin with his finger and forces her to look into his eyes. Fear eats at his soul. "Ask her," he implores the linguist. "Ask her when she went into the cave."

"Keen wy es hera en box?" the linguist says.

Quinn's eyes lock onto Natalia.

"Hundo fuin heinte," she whispers.

"She says, the time of the third king," the linguist says.

The linguist crawls to her, his mouth a thin line of despair. He asks her more questions, his frame now leaning against Quinn's. They both listen as she talks, whispering as tears fall down her cheeks.

"Her people lived in a different time," the linguist says. "They tracked time differently, you see. She speaks of a time of New

Fire." He pulls on his mouth, his eyebrows squinting in confusion. "If my memory serves me correctly, the Anaxian dialect, the third King, and New Fire ceremony trail back hundreds and hundreds of years."

"Hundreds of years? You 're telling me that she thinks she has been here for hundreds of years?" Darius doesn't hide the contempt in his voice. He stands five feet back from the others, his arms crossed over his chest.

"That's what it would seem. Yes."

No one responds to him. Minutes pass before anyone else speaks. Natalia continues to cry as the men gaze at her and one by one they retreat. One by one, they walk away from the hole to the cave and leave her to mourn.

Quinn is not sure how long they let her sit. He, too, sits while he waits for her. Hours pass before he finally hears footsteps behind him.

"She is sick, Quinn. We can't help her out here. We can't even understand her," Bailey says.

Quinn paces back and forth in front of the unlit fire. The moisture of the air thickens on his skin.

"They'll take her to a doctor, help her figure out what happened. They'll help her work through whatever devastation or confusion she faced."

"Let me go with her. Comodoro Rivadavia is a huge oil town. I will be fine getting a place to stay while they figure it out for her," Quinn says.

"Absolutely not. Your mother would turn in her grave if she knew I was listening to such an absurd idea. We don't even know her. We don't know a damn thing about her!"

"That's the point, Pops. No one does. Three days. It's been

three damn days and forgive me, but I think we are the only ones she has!" His voice stretches across the ground and he lowers it. "This isn't like back home. What the hell will happen to her in a mental ward when no one comes to claim her, and no one is able to find out the truth? What will happen to her then?"

"But what if someone does come, Quinn?" Bailey says. "It's entirely possible. It could be her only chance of someone finding her." He pauses and looks at Quinn with sympathy in his eyes. "She is sick. It's entirely possible she put herself in that cave."

"Three days. She has been sleeping and eating with us for three days. Have you ever once thought her screwed in the head? Have you ever once thought her actions bizarre or hazardous to herself or anyone else? Think about it, Pops. It doesn't make any sense." He paces, anger and frustration bubbling in his chest.

"And sleeping in a cave for hundreds of years does?" Bailey runs his hand over the length of his face and pauses to look at the girl staring into the forest. "We finish out here, veer into the woods as much as we can. Then we will go. Then we go to Comodoro Rivadavia."

Quinn nods, accepting that it is the best offer he will get, and turns his back on his father. He strides past the officials busily making plans for her transport, while Darius and Ryan share detail after detail with the linguist. Her trunk has been moved to the back of the Jeep. The linguist closely examines Natalia's sketches.

Quinn approaches Natalia. Her face is strained as she gazes into the forest. He sits down in front of her, softly brushing the hair from her face.

Her eyes grieve as she turns to him. So solemn. Hollowed out by rare emotion.

"They are going to take you. They are going to do the only thing they know how to try and help you."

She silently cries as he talks.

He hopes in his heart she understands what he is trying to tell her. "A few months. Give us a few months, and we will come. As soon as I can, I will come for you." He squeezes her hand to reassure not only her, but himself as well.

The officials arrive. They help her to her feet. Her eyebrows squint and she dries the tears on her face.

He, too, rises to his feet and follows behind as they head away. She walks with them but keeps her head turned, her eyes locked on him.

Her head snaps back and forth between Quinn and the Jeep, alarm awakening in her eyes. She understands what is going on.

"Quinn?" she says. "Quinn!"

"I'm sorry, Natalia. I'm so sorry!" He stops just out of reach from the jeep's rear end. The officials keep walking her forward.

"Quinn!"

Her body pushes against the officials to reach him. "Quinn!"

As she is escorted into the Jeep, her legs give way. Picking her up, they force her into the Jeep and strap her into the back. She turns to find him through the back window. Her eyes plead with him to stop them. Stop them from taking her. Her teeth bite the corner of her lips. The linguist sits next to her, and she starts to cry once more, her eyes nestled on Quinn. And just as leisurely as they came, the officials drive her away.

Chapter Ten
Natalia

I am not an ignorant girl. I know why they took me. I know what the two uniformed men think of me. But I also know that the linguist doubts them.

When they leave me in the care of the doctors, he stays. He talks me through their machines and physical exams. He translates my story and shakes his head with each new detail.

What I do not know is how to understand their machines and their technology as they describe it. But I try my best to cooperate and study the pictures of my brain along with them. I push my pain down deep in my heart and try to hold strong. I brace myself for the quizzical glares and harsh prodding.

The doctors study the strange pictures over and over again, then ask for my story one last time. They want to know about the guards who put me in the cave. They want to know why I went so willingly. They want to know the answers to things I myself am beginning to doubt. Could it really have been that long ago? Was any of it real? My memory tells me I was taken to live in isolation when I was barely old enough to walk in shoes. But could it have all been a trick? An illusion? I was meant to be protected from the evils of the world and kept pure at all costs. But maybe, just maybe, could I be remembering it wrong?

They want to know about the dragon. How could a dragon disappear? Where could it possibly have gone? I know they don't believe me. Each one of their questions becomes thicker and thicker with accusations. No matter what had happened to me, they doubt my stories of the dark. I know I would be better off If I stopped talking to them and let my story die. But Santino, the linguist, urges me on with his sweet encouragement and trust.

So, they put me in yet another cave, the only difference being the white padded walls and the metal-framed bed. Maybe. Just maybe I truly am crazy. How could I not be with the world's shape around me? I try to search for proof. Some sort of explanation. But I find none. My soul is completely empty.

Santino pleads with me. "You have to get out of bed, my dear. The longer you stay in bed, I fear the longer you will be kept inside this room." He scratches at the scruff on his chin, his round cheeks flush with red.

"There is nothing, Santino. So I sleep. There is nothing more to do."

"Ah, but you are wrong. There is life. You need to get out of bed, and you need to live it." Sitting on the edge of my small cot, he picks up my palm and rests it in his.

I move my weight to one side, tasting the blood in my mouth from the new habit of biting my cheek. "My life is gone, Santino. This is all that remains. I was delivered to sleep. So I take it."

"Until you make it more, my dear. You hold the key. You find out your past, or you choose to make a future. You decide."

"What is life without a past? They are telling me it was all a dream, and yet I can remember nothing else. How do you walk forward if there is nothing behind you?"

"Then make it today. Walk away from today. Leave today behind and never look back."

Never look back. Father had told me something similar once. It had been a hard winter of war, and he was intent on riding out the next day.

"It's my fault, Father," I had confessed to him. "I brought this war upon us."

His eyebrows had scrunched as he gazed at me as I pleaded. "My sacrifice was not large enough. My thoughts of the empire were not pure. Let them fight their own battles. Stay here with me."

"My little queen, we look forward. We look at what needs to be done for tomorrow. We each have a purpose," he had said. "And *your purpose* is for tomorrow. Remember that and never look back."

"Santino," I say. "Do you think me crazy?"

"Crazy is a stupid word. The world is full of crazies, yet you are the only one stuck in this room."

"But, do you think me crazy?" I squeeze his fingers in my own.

His held tilts and his eyes soften towards mine. "No, my dear. No, I do not."

"Then teach me, Santino. Teach me their language and help me make tomorrow my purpose."

Chapter Eleven
Quinn

Five months. Bailey and Quinn took five months before they pulled the old Jeep into the dusty parking lot. Natalia wasn't very hard to find, not after asking for the girl with memories of a life that was an archeological reverie. She had been moved from the hospital just over four months ago. Santino Malino followed behind shortly thereafter.

Now, standing in front of the old, refurbished institution with brick walls and white shutters, Santino looks far more professional, far more sober. He is dressed in white linen slacks with his shirt buttoned loosely over his belly. The same sandals fit his feet. Although his face is clean from ruffage, his eyes hold the same urgency, the same rushed panic as they had five months prior.

"She talks nothing of it," Santino says. "Neither of her cave nor what existed in her prior life. She has been diagnosed with Psychogenic Amnesia." He pauses and lights his pipe. "They concluded that she had an extremely traumatic or violent experience that shut down her brain's ability to process it. An act of self-preservation, if you will, repressing not only her memories but also her identity … blocked in her subconscious, merely waiting to be lifted."

They walk around the four-story building with peeling paint, following a path to a small courtyard at the back.

The sun sits high in the sky and Santino wipes his sweating brow. "When her short-term memories began forming once more, she was confused and began verbalizing a false history that very well could have been fed to her or perhaps dreamed up."

They stop walking near a small stream covered in ivy and lupines. Natalia is staring at the water, slowly plucking petals off the flowers and tossing them into the water. Her skin shines, translucent in the heat of the air. Her feet remain bare, her shoulders exposed to the sun.

"The problem," Santino continues, "is that all of her procedural memories were gone. Simple things like plumbing had to be explained and re-taught. Foods and their origins were alien to her. Electricity. She once asked me how we trapped the sun in the glass of a lightbulb." He smiled at the memory and looked up at the girl with longing.

"What does all of this mean to you, Santino? What is your opinion?" Bailey says.

He is quiet as he considers his answer and looks around impatiently. "I think she is holding back. I think there are more truths she holds only to herself. The weight on her shoulders may bear a lot of things, but I do not think it stole her memories."

Bailey and Quinn listen with intrigue. Quinn bites his tongue to keep from interrupting.

"Her father, for example. If you catch her in the right moment, she can describe him in perfect detail and share memories that bring tears to her eyes. Although my mind screams at me, my heart hurts for her. Even if it is not the truth, it remains her truth." He starts walking toward the girl, then turns back to the two men.

"She learned English in three months. The doctors tell me that it is proof the language was there the whole time, and simply found its way out." He takes a long and deliberate smoke.

"What do you think?" Quinn says.

He pauses once more. The cascading stream drowns out his silence. "I think…I think it was the only thing she had left to fight for. It was her only hope."

"Why would English be her only hope? She is in a country that speaks almost entirely Spanish."

"Because of you, my friends. You speak English, and she thinks you are her only hope."

Quinn considers this as he studies the girl, his stomach clenching as he absorbs her beauty once more. The soft green sundress hangs off one shoulder and flows down to her bare feet.

His heart fills with longing, much as it does for Santino at his side. For different reasons, perhaps. Or perhaps not. The girl is a marvel. As she turns to gaze at her audience, her chin points to the sky. Her eyebrows rise and her lips tighten in a purposeful line.

The approach of the petite girl lightens Quinn's feet, and he catches his breath. He holds in the hope he finds in her, in the beauty cascading off her face and deep into the crevasses of his heart.

Stopping next to Santino, she curtsies at the two men now in front of her. "Very nice to see you, Mr. Bailey, Mr. Quinn."

Even with the English lessons, her accent remains thick with rolling consonants. It sends shivers down Quinn's spine. Months of anticipation suddenly leave him speechless.

"We found something, Natalia. We think it might belong to you." Bailey pulls the small wooden carving out of his pocket, rubbing it anxiously between his thumb and forefinger.

Taking the small carving, she smiles and her eyes water. She pulls the delicate obsidian chain over her head, leaving the small pine carving cupped in her hand.

"My father carved it for me. He always referred to me as his precious chestnut." Her eyes never leave the small piece of wood. "Chestnuts are unique. Their spiny shell is reminiscent of a spur that sticks to your skin and the slender remains hidden within."

Her eyes remain lost in memories the others could not reach.

"Have you ever had a chestnut, Natalia?" Bailey says.

Her tortured eyes pull away from the wood and meet his. "No. They did not grow in my territory. Or at least they did not at the time. But my father, he traveled far. His stories of the world always traveled home with him."

She drops the small carving and nods at Bailey. "Thank you. Mr. Bailey. This heirloom is very precious to me." Her eyes meet his, and she curtsies once more.

"Of course, Natalia."

Bailey squints at her with questions etched on his face. "Your English is beautiful. How? How is that possible?"

"That, too, Mr. Bailey. That, too, is a treasure. They tell me English was trapped inside. Just as a chestnut perhaps, merely waiting to be broken out."

"Do you believe them?" Quinn says.

She tilts her head but does not respond. "I have waited very patiently for you to arrive, Mr. Bailey. I always knew you would come." She turns to look at Quinn and questions him with her eyes. "I need your help. Please. If there is any way to take me with you, I will do whatever you ask. I can learn to cook or help you dig. Whatever it is you need, I can learn."

"You want to come with us to our next dig site, or you want us to get you out of here?"

"Both. Both, I suppose. I am not sick. Lost maybe. But what they say about me, it is not the truth. Even Mr. Santino knows this is not the truth. He may not say it, but he knows." Her body turns to face her ally, determination strong in her stance. "Isn't that right, Mr. Santino?"

The emotions on her face press into Quinn's own emotions.

Santino looks at her with sad admiration. "No. No, I don't believe you are sick, miss. But you are also underage with no understandable history. No family to claim you, and no memories you claim as your own. I fear you will not be allowed to leave without due course, ma'am. And if you are, it would take a miracle."

They all stare at the dirt at their feet in silence.

"Give me a few days, Natalia. Just a few days. And when the time comes, you play along. The best you know how. I'll help you. And then you can come help us," Bailey says.

"How, Mr. Bailey? I do not understand."

"Just trust that we will help. Can you do that?"

"Yes. Thank you. Thank you, Mr. Bailey. Thank you."

Quinn and his father are silent as they walk back to their jeep. It isn't until Quinn opens the passenger door that he turns towards his father. "Why didn't you tell him, Pops? Or even her? Why didn't you tell her about the wood?"

"Carbon dating is irrelevant to her. She holds those memories regardless of their age. It's us who needed convincing. Not her."

Quinn nods his head as they drive off in silence. He holds onto unwavering hope and resolve as they leave the 800-year-old artifact behind.

Chapter Twelve
Natalia

I am sitting in the foyer watching the leaves brush past the window screen when a man enters the main door behind me. His feet are soft, unsure.

"Excuse me, miss?" The man is hesitant. "I was hoping you could help me. I was looking for my sister. One of the nurses from the National Arzobispo Loayza Hospital told me she thinks she was sent here. Her name is Natalia. She has been missing for six months now."

My body tenses as I overhear the conversation, and my head instantly snaps to see the nurse's reaction.

"Sí! Sí Señor, Sí! Natalia! Natalia!"

The head caretaker is frantic as she moves swiftly to the foyer and lifts me from my seat. Her grip is strong and her force mighty.

Ryan stands with both hands pushed into the beige pockets of his pants. Although I don't quite know what to say, I am positive recognition flashes across my face.

He runs to me, embraces me in a wrap that tangles my entire frame against his chest. Heart pounding, still slightly confused, I feel my body relax in his embrace. I feel his assurances that everything will be alright. And for the first time in months, I feel safe, like the demons of my mind are no longer hunting me.

"My God! What happened to you? I turned around for one second and you were gone! What the hell happened to you?"

He pulls me away and stares into my face, but I don't know what to say. I don't know how to play this game of his and am terrified of speaking up and ruining it. Slowly turning his head back to the caretaker, his eyebrows scrunch. "What's wrong with her?"

"We believe she fell. Or was distressed greatly. There are no memories. Although it is a good sign that she recognizes you. Once her memories start to come back, we feel assured it will be swift."

"What do I need to do? I want to take her home."

I am sent upstairs to gather my belongings while Ryan takes care of the medical semantics of my stay. Aside from the bill, they do not care where I go or who I leave with. Although I am grateful, it makes me wonder if I could have slipped out on my own, if only I had a place to go. I pack my belongings into a bag and hang it over my shoulder. I stare at the dirty old trunk at my feet. It holds nothing more for me. I shouldn't care if it stays or goes, but my heart beats faster than it should. It is just one more thing in my life I must leave behind.

With my belongings secure in one small shoulder bag, I exit the room. If only I had a chance to say goodbye to Santino, but surely he will know. He will know how I feel and understand. I have no doubt he will know where I have gone.

Ryan squeezes my hand as we walk to the Jeep. Much as a brother would, I suppose. His appearance has softened since the last time I saw him. His face is smooth and his brown hair tucks neatly behind his ears. Forgetting his age, I assume he is about ten years my senior. He carries himself much as one of my past tutors had. Educated. Aware. Protective. He takes the pack off my shoulder to carry it himself. He opens the door to the Jeep and helps lift me into the passenger seat. The door is closed as soon as I am safely fastened inside. My head turns back to the caretaker waving behind the screen of the house. I do not wave back.

We drive in silence for several hours, yet conversation is not missed. Silence remains comfortable, expected even. My insides feel clouded, though. Anxious. When the sun finally begins to set, we approach a moderately-sized villa with a flat, square roof and greenery growing randomly in front of the sunken windows. There is no stone or marble, nor a castle. No resemblance to anything I have ever seen. Yet the house looks exquisite.

Inside, wooden banisters cover the length of the house from the floor to the ceiling. Stairs with banisters caressing the natural curve of the steps rise to bedchambers at the highest level of the villa. To the left of the stairs, a great room opens up to living quarters, resplendent with cotton sofas and pillows overflowing from each piece of furniture. A wall of windows covers the room in light, and the wooden floors shine.

Bailey, Quinn, and Darius all rise to their feet as I enter the room. Smiles spread across their faces and my heart instantly fills. They are pleased at my arrival. It fills my heart with so much joy. It makes me feel wanted. Missed and remembered. Simply being.

"Come, sit, sit." Mr. Bailey rushes to my side and escorts me to the soft sofa. "How are you? How did it go?" His voice rambles in excitement, leaving us little room to answer all of his questions.

"Too easy." Ryan places my few belongings next to the door. "Expensive, but otherwise easy."

Bailey smiles at me. His eyes are soft and filled with admiration. "That's quite alright."

Quinn leans over and rests his arms on his knees. His eyes never leave me, but I don't seem to have the courage to return the stare. He, too, is smiling. He, too, is pleased at my arrival.

"We would like you to start at the beginning, Natalia, knowing your story is safe. Safe with every one of us. In order to know how to move forward, we want you to be able to trust us," Mr. Bailey says.

"I do trust you, Mr. Bailey. But I need to know why. Why do you help me as you do?"

He remains silent for only a moment, then looks at Quinn for confirmation. "My wife was an orphan. Even in her death, her spirit wouldn't allow me to leave you alone."

My fingers brush the hair behind both my ears. The curls bounce in the smooth motion. My shoulders pull up and my head tilts to the side. "Her spirit? Does her spirit remain with you now?"

"Um, yes, I suppose she does."

"I grew up believing that once we passed, our spirits passed on as well, reborn into a better life filled with higher hopes and fewer obligations."

I stand apprehensively and move to touch the cotton-stuffed furniture, the wooden coffee table, and the glass lamp resting on an end table. "A life where the spirits of the deceased stay with me for guidance seems much more appealing." Stopping to finger the keys on the grand piano, I close my eyes. "I miss my father greatly. To think of his soul in a body I am unable to reach saddens my heart."

Quinn speaks up. "What can we do for you, Natalia? Can we help you?"

I straighten my shoulders as I try to fain confidence. It used to be there all the time. So sturdy. Secure. It was all a queen ever needed. But now I need it more than ever, and I have to pull at it from the tips of my grasp. I face the four men, all of them now seated, taking me in. Listening. Trusting. "I need you to take me to Estancia."

"Estancia has been a myth on this continent for decades," Darius says. "We wouldn't know how or where to start."

"It's believed to be a desolate landscape covered in gold," Ryan says. "If it's out there, I think someone would have found it by now."

A small smile brightens my face. "It's there. I just need a map, and I'll get you there. Any riches along the way will be yours to keep."

"What do you hope to find there?" Quinn says.

"Answers. I need answers."

Chapter Thirteen
Quinn

Bailey and Darius begin making lists of supplies for their journey ahead, and Ryan leaves to find a map without roads or highways, just the empty terrain. Natalia is put in Quinn's charge, and sent to town to find what Bailey refers to as *appropriate* hiking clothes.

They take advantage of the time allowed and choose to walk to town rather than taking the Jeep. They walk side by side on the dirt roads. Quinn shuffles his feet with his hands safely secured inside his pant pockets. With his eyes keeping track of his feet, he only looks to steal soft smiles and glances from Natalia.

Unlike him, she does not walk as if she is trying to keep her hands from fidgeting. Her shoulders stand tall as she walks, her feet soft, refusing to displace any of the dirt from the road. Her gaze scours the countryside. Her gazes crosses every inch of the sky.

At first, he worries the walk might be too long for her. But she never stops to complain. Her body never hints towards fatigue.

Quinn escorts her to a busy street near the town square. People crowd the dirt roads and push past one another without thinking. Their eyes transfix on the people around them without ever truly seeing anything. Bicycles move between the sidewalks and streets, and children run through the crowds shrieking in play.

Natalia's head remains high with the confidence he imagines as falsified, or maybe even trained. Her eyes touch everything the square has to offer, from the ceramic tiles to the glass pottery, the velvet cushions to the oiled artwork. He imagines her own artwork displayed there as well. She would be a success and greatly profit from her talent.

"How are you doing, Natalia?" He finally has the courage to ask. His question lingers in the air, for he is asking so much more than just the words that rest at his lips.

She stops at a cart of fabrics to fold the linen of a shawl through her fingertips. Her eyes reach up to notice how it is hung in a display before pulling her eyes down to meet his. "I feel lost," she says. "I am in a body that is my own in a world that is not." She attempts a smile but finds little curve to the structure of her lips.

"Is everything new to you?" he says.

"Not necessarily new. Just confusing. I know nothing of how or why anything is. I know not of the food or supplies that fill up space. Only of the sun. The stars. The sound of my feet walking on the ground, and the emptiness of my heart."

"What do you miss the most, Natalia?" His voice is quiet, as if he is scared to hear her answer.

"Hope." She states it simply and walks away from the merchant's stand as if it were a mere apple core left in the road. She turns her head back at him, finally finding her true smile, and silently urges him to keep up.

He imagines her hope like a mirage. Trailing in the distance, too far from her grasp. Although he wants to ask more, her lingering smile tells him she will once she is ready. He can wait until then. He can wait as long as she needs.

He ignores the temptation of the square and is left with only the temptation her body holds so near to his own. When brushing past her, heat radiates to his heart, leaving the hair on his arms quivering for more. His breath comes out hard and heavy. Ashamed, he holds onto the air pulled into his lungs and pledges his soul to hide his attraction for her. His knees become wobbly and his voice quakes as he asks her time and time again if any of the square displays interest her. There are no simple gowns like the one Natalia now wears.

She smiles at him, showing the smallest of dimples under her left cheek. "Neh," she says. "Not yet."

She stops once more outside a cantina. Dozens of people busy themselves with day-to-day matters and conversations, all while Natalia stares at the circled sidewalk in the square. A great stone dragon with talons made of plaster entices her. The stonework is old, cracked, and flawed from years of people walking over its intricate design. Reds flame with the bricks and black is forged into each stone, making its color more vibrant than the stonework that lay around it.

At first, she merely circles around it. Squinting her eyes as if she is thinking it through, he watches her. Deep in thought.

She ignores the people in the square and drops to her knees to trace the design. Measured and deliberate, her index finger traces the outline of the untamed beast. Crawling on all fours, she bends to reach the whip of its tail, her hand moving back toward the dragon's head. Opening her palm, her hair falls to cover the jaw of the giant beast. Lowering her chin, her eyes close. Sadness pours out of her like water from a pitcher.

Quinn's heart aches for her, yet his unease enables him to move closer. He recalls her sketches of the dragon made of stone. He refrains from bending down to reach for her. To comfort her in an embrace.

She begins to sing.

Lifelong hunt is far and wide,

Sacrifice, no longer at her side.

Born again, save my king,

Take my breath, hear me sing.

Rejoice in loss, blood drips cold,

Till the dragon, her bounty sold.

He took it all, fire and life,

Her heart lay pierced without the knife.

Her silent tears drip to the pavement.

Quinn musters the courage and encircles her waist with his arms. He pulls her to her feet. He faces her, his body inches from her own. Cupping her face with his left hand, he wipes away her tears with the other. "Is your dragon real?" he whispers, almost too frightened to hear the answer.

"Yes. Yes, Quinn, he is."

His face inches closer to her, his lips soaking in the moisture her breath has to offer. Yet he stalls and pulls back just enough to see the square has emptied.

It is enough to alert him that something is wrong. Out of place. The hairs on the back of his neck raise, and his muscles stiffen with apprehension. Natalia, too, has dropped her hold on Quinn, and stares across the walkway with confusion heavy in her weight.

Two men shadow the base of the stone walkway. One is older than his forefathers, with skin wrinkled deep. His bones scream malnourishment and he holds a wooden cane to support his posture. Standing humbled, shoulders hunched with age, his hair grows in random strands across his face. But it is his eyes that force Quinn to stumble back from Natalia. Eyes of rage, eyes of a warrior.

Natalia grabs Quinn's wrist as he attempts to retreat. Fear penetrates through her fingers. "It isn't possible," she whispers.

"Do you know him?" Quinn says.

Her grip on his arm tightens. "We must leave. This isn't right."

Cleanly dressed in black slacks and a white button-down shirt, the second man sits on a bench ten feet behind the old crow. His black hair radiates blue at the tips that flash in the light of the sun. His face reflects mockery, and he smiles wickedness. He stands and saunters over to the old man.

His eyes drill into Natalia as he whispers into the old man's ear. The old man stomps his cane to the ground and points it directly at Natalia. The old man continues to stare at Natalia, knowingly, with hatred filling his eyes.

Rolling his eyes slightly at the old man, the younger man begins to approach Natalia and Quinn. His feet are heavy, filling the air with the sound of each step. He carries resentment in his strides, and annoyance across his features.

"There is rumor of a girl in these parts. A girl snatched up by dragons. A girl with song in her voice and olive on her skin." Taking a step closer, his eyes soften. A dare leaks into his voice. "My grandfather here thinks that girl to be you."

Natalia stands modestly beside Quinn. Her touch burns into his soul. "That is impossible," she whispers.

The young man takes another step closer, as if fearful of scaring them off. "Is it you? Are you the lost sacrifice?"

"There are many girls. Many girls who sing. Many with my skin," she whispers.

"But there are not many, I suppose, who have dragon magic running through their veins." As he steps closer, Quinn steps forward and shields Natalia's small frame behind his shoulders. "Can you prove it?" the young stranger says. "Because if you can't, my grandfather will not rest. He will not stop until he knows it is not you."

"I come from the villa up the road. What your grandfather speaks of is nonsense. Come, Quinn, come." She pulls on his wrists. "We must make our purchases before nightfall. Come."

He responds to the urgency in her voice, the persistence of her touch, and follows her out of the square. The two men stand as statues and watch them leave. Neither speaks and neither moves to follow them across the square. Quinn silently questions their deliberate confrontation, their motives, and unspoken desires. But mostly he questions Natalia's fears. Why would she be afraid of a familiar face? Why would she not embrace such men if they thought they knew her or the truth about her past? Despite her search for answers, she ran away from them awfully fast.

They walk hand in hand a half dozen blocks, always looking behind. Natalia no longer speaks of dragons or hope and shattered dreams. She no longer speaks at all.

They find their way into a corner store. Shutters painted in orange surround both the windows as well as the front door to the shop. It smells like paprika and seems to relax Natalia instantly. She rummages through each part of the store and gathers each of her choice of product into her arms. They buy pants, boots, even socks for her. She laughs at the fashion while rubbing the bottoms of her feet. Little by little, her mood begins to lighten once more. Little by little, Quinn feels at ease enough to follow suit. He sheepishly asks the young woman in charge to supply her with woman's things. The store clerk's eyes widen, but she does his bidding.

Secluded and detached from the wearisome strangers they had encountered earlier, Natalia transforms into a new girl of the twenty-first century. She chooses to keep her green sun dress on, but Quinn laces up her new black leather boots and carries the bags as they leave.

His eyes are distracted by the jade lace on her dress as it falls down the side of her bare shoulder. The smell of eucalyptus lingers in her trail, and that of his shuddering heart, only a few feet behind.

"Did you know them, Natalia?" Quinn asks on the way home.

"No. No, I didn't."

"It kind of looked like they knew you."

"It's nonsense," she states plainly. "I cannot be who they seek."

Chapter Fourteen
Natalia

Back at the house, I find my self-assurance once more while showing off my new favorite accessories, my black leather boots. The laces hold my admiration with the thick footing on the soles, and the ankle protection thick on the sides. My delicate slippers had never allowed such anomalies.

"Those are fighting boots," Mr. Bailey says, amusement glinting in his eyes.

I blink at him in confusion. "Do women fight here?"

"Yes, yes I suppose they do."

Mr. Bailey stands up and with little effort moves the small coffee table to the side. "Come, let me teach you the basics."

"Ney, Mr. Bailey you are very kind, but it would have been forbidden." I drop my head, shame sweeping over me. Even my eyelids bear the weight.

"Exactly." He hurries to my side. He slips his index finger under the tip of my chin, forcing me lift my eyes to meet his own. "Would have been. That is no longer the case."

I nod in understanding, but still question it in my heart. It's confusing how the world changes over time. How fighting boots and acts of aggression could be displayed by nearly everyone, and emotion can be so publicly displayed. My behavior in the square today would have been reason enough to throw me over a cliff. A queen never should have touched another in public. But as Mr. Bailey states, then and now are different things. Yet my mind is still trying to make clarifications on which is which.

Quinn enters the room, popping the lid off the drink in his hand. "Teach her right, old man. Or I'll have to show her how it's really done." Taking a seat on the empty sofa, a smirk spreads across his face.

Mr. Bailey doesn't take his eyes off me, but his eyebrows rise. "Who do you think taught that boy everything he knows?"

I smile and nod my head.

Mr. Bailey takes my fingers into his own and curls them around my palm. "Never tuck your thumb in. Hold it tightly to secure the other fingers, else it might break."

My eyes go wide. "I do not think I will have that kind of strength, Mr. Bailey."

"Trust that you might and keep that thumb out. That's all that matters."

As Mr. Bailey helps set my feet into proper position and trains my arm to soar in the appropriate direction, I feel Quinn's gaze held to me. His stare feeds me deeper than the feeling of abandonment, deeper than the years of anger held so tightly inside. His eyes glimmer at me, forcing my pulse to grow stronger and my skin flush.

After an hour, Mr. Bailey moves on to kicks, allowing my eagerness to use my new boots for their true intent. It makes my legs feel aggressive and strong, encouraging each kick more than the swing of my arms.

By the time our lesson is over, my face drips with perspiration and I am silently mortified. A queen should never be seen perspiring, I whisper in my head. And then I stop to look back up at Mr. Bailey. That was then, he had said. Not now. I gratefully accept the towel and cold bottled water Quinn offers.

"Maybe we should hit the showers…." His voice trails off into a whisper.

"Quinn!" Mr. Bailey yells.

"What? I'm a teenage boy. What do you expect? That was hot!"

"I'm sorry, Mr. Quinn, I did not mean to offend." More embarrassment blankets over me, and the smirk on Quinn's face broadens.

"No, Natalia, I'm sorry. I meant it as a compliment. A compliment to your beauty. A compliment to your badass boots."

Taking a deep breath, I remind myself of now, not then. I remind myself of my new purpose. The people in my midst and the dragon of my past. "I would like it to be more than just the boots that are bad ass." I smile and nod at his deep eyes. "Thank you for the lesson, Mr. Bailey." I make her way to the shower just as Quinn suggested.

I let the water drench my hair and feel the desire build under my skin. A desire so strong it humbles me. Never in my life have I felt such a thing, not the warmth under my skin or even the sharpness of my breath. Not only do I ignore all of my upbringing, but I also find enjoyment from the enticement. What would Father have said with such delicate feet swinging towards an unarmed man? A man twice my size, nevertheless, teaching me how to fight. Swinging my fists into the air, my strength tugs at the anger they help release.

Far worse, I think of Quinn. I think of his eyes on me, longing for them to stay there. I long for his arms wrapped around my waist. Just as they were when he pulled me from the cave. Just the same as when holding me in town. I wish for the smile to linger, the smile always intended for me. But I was raised that such thoughts were forbidden. I had always known my destiny. Known the nature of what my survival would entail. Even that of my death. Or what my death should have entailed.

Men looking at me or me looking at them was never a pleasure I expected or accepted. They would have been hanged for such an action. And me? I would have been drowned in the river, cleansed of my impure thoughts, disgraced by my family and disgraced by the king.

But now, now I am not so sure. I feel lost, questioning all I have ever known. I think of the men who stole me from my destiny and delivered me to the dragon's lair. Surely, they found their own deaths. Their choices would have ensured it. Now I am in a place contrary to my lost life, in a world where girls wear boots and fight men. A world where I am left thinking of Quinn while I cleanse my own impurity away with the impure thoughts and impure desires for the young man who sleeps in the room adjacent to my own.

How twisted to be raised so far away from the temptation of man, to now be so close to one that I can hear him breathing as he sleeps. The dragon was far less torturous.

Chapter Fifteen
Quinn

Ryan plays the piano the next morning as Bailey prepares breakfast.

Quinn hangs on each note, absorbing the memory of melodies his mother would have loved. He stands in the hall with his eyes closed, remembering this exact moment. Ten years prior maybe, but still, the memory rips at his flesh.

"Make it more upbeat!" he says. "Before I kill myself."

Ryan's soft waltz pauses, forcing a smile on Quinn's face. He knows Ryan favors the classical shit, but also knows his drive for acceptance. The beat picks up as Natalia rounds the corner. Bailey starts to sing in the kitchen, an awful tune ransacked with off key notes painstakingly trying to keep up with Ryan's new melody.

Darius comes into the room dancing. He drops a container of orange juice on the side table and spins toward the piano. His socks slide against the wooden floor. He dances with his arms over his head, his knees twisting apart then together again. Ryan picks the beat up once more.

A smile crosses Quinn's face as Bailey enters the room, spatula up to his mouth, singing nonsensical onomatopoeias. "Oh my God, you guys are so embarrassing." He shakes his head, a palm flat over his eyes.

Natalia covers her mouth, but a giggle escapes. Bailey slides over to the hall, taking Natalia's sheepish hands in his own. He slows, with a patience only a father could hold, and allows her to learn the bounce of the rhythm. Her knees start with the motion, unsure, and apprehensive. Her hips move next, graciously flowing from one side to the next.

But it isn't the knees or even the hips that grab Quinn's attention. Not the hand stretched toward Quinn or the smile on her face. It's the roomful of adults, the family that fills up his thoughts. It's the music. It's the music he asked for with a family he can call his own. And a girl. A girl who holds the music in her eyes before the slide of her feet. A girl with bad ass fighting boots, untied and dangling dangerously on the floor as she steps side to side.

He does what anyone in his position would do. He takes her outstretched hand, buries his pride, and begins to dance with his crazy makeshift family. He spins and moves from side to side. He lets his dad carry on to a made-up song and joins Ryan's rhythm.

The jug of orange juice, passed around the room like a pipe, lies empty by the time they are finished. Ryan flexes his fingers, pulling them back to rest behind his head as he sprawls out on the floor.

The others follow, exhaustion taking over their jubilee. Quinn's hand locks in Natalia's as they breathe in the room, the smell of burnt bacon quickly filling up the surrounding space. Timid and soft, a little unsure, her fingers lace between his. Her eyes dart to his and pull away just as quickly.

"Your music is splendid, Mr. Ryan," Natalia says. "How did you learn to play?"

"I went to camps as a kid. My parents traveled, so I spent a lot of time bouncing from one place to another. When I was about ten, I went to this music camp just outside New Mexico." Ryan sits up and crosses his legs. "The camp had two things I fell in love with: piano and dirt." He smiles at her. "When us kids weren't busy with lessons, we were free to roam around the desert. That's when I started digging." Lying down, he rests his hands behind his neck. "Not only did I come home that year with talent but also dozens of rocks, fossils, and maybe even a few animal bones." He closes his eyes, lost in thought. "I never chose to go to another camp again."

"Did they travel away to wars? Your parents?" Natalia says.

"No, not my parents. They went to parties. Work functions. That sort of thing." He turns his head to smirk at Bailey. "I see Bailey more than I see them."

"That's only because of all the dirt I surround myself in," Bailey says.

"Nah," Darius says. "It's 'cause Bailey is the pops you never knew you wanted."

"And the dirt," Quinn says.

"What about you, Mr. Darius? How did you come to be here?"

"Bailey was the only professor I ever had who gave me A's. I figured I needed to stick around." He stands up, moving toward the kitchen. "Six years later, I'm still here." He throws away the remnants of the burnt bacon and opens up the fridge to pull out a fresh supply. "When do we leave anyway?"

"Tomorrow." Bailey rolls to his knees and stands. "Let's get everything ready today. We can leave in the morning."

Natalia's grip tightens on Quinn's fingers. As the warmth of her fingers spreads to his own, he can't help but feel the fear building in her gut. Her anxiousness about the journey spreads to him, but he laughs at the unknown and moves to help with the bacon.

Chapter Sixteen
Natalia

I have no idea what I am doing. My pack lies heavy on my back and the bedroll hangs awkwardly at its side. My thoughts run to alpacas: how alpacas should be carrying all of this for me and I shouldn't have to be responsible for packing it. Never would I have imagined men carrying their own belongings without the help of an animal. Never would I have imagined carrying my own bags without servants. My eyes dart to the packs on each of those trudging ahead of me. Twice the size of my pack, theirs hold weaponry, nourishment, and medicines. And knowledge. They hold much more knowledge.

My legs aren't used to this much exercise, and within hours I feel like rubber. But I do not slow. And I will not fall back. If my answers lie ahead, then ahead is where I must go.

We walk on the edge of the forest, listening to the songs of the birds calling to me. They whistle tunes of encouragement. Not just to me, but to all of us. My feet carry me over the shrubbery. I let the branches thrash against my ankles as I embrace the thickness of the forest. The softness of the leaves tickles my skin and the occasional bite of a thorn sticks to my pants. Leaves rustle. Branches snap. The cicadas sing. The sounds of the forest bring back childhood memories, and I am a child of the forest once more. Free from the expectations of villagers. Free from prosperity. Free from the weight of my unfilled promises.

We stop at dusk to make camp with our only protection from the campfire. From what I know of the animals in these parts, a fire may not be enough to warn them off. There are far more dangerous things in the forest than things that prowl. Then again, the brutality of the weaponry each man holds at his side may be more than sufficient. I refuse a handgun, but settle for a dagger small enough to wrap into my skirt. Although Mr. Ryan insists, I wear pants underneath for I favor the flow of the skirts hanging at my side.

The dagger goes untouched. Day after day. Hike after hike. I end up forgetting it's there and focus my attention on Estancia. Only once did I grow apprehensive about our direction, fearing the land had changed too much over the course of time. But holding true to men's maps, I am sure our destination lies ahead.

The songs of the jungle are soothing. In the songs of the birds, the crunching leaves of the mammals, or even the chirps of the bugs' symphony. They all float together with the wind and the rustle of the leaves. I focus on the whistling music of the animals in the sky.

I lose count of the days and look forward to the cover of night under familiar stars that never falter. The friendly lights where I am watched over in my sleep, warm by the fire. I can fall into the darkness, free from the confines of a cave, the confines of white padded walls, or the unfamiliar wooden floors that sparkle in the sunshine.

Quinn brings me courage. When darkness overtakes me, I am free to stare in admiration without discovery. We smile at each other before sleep overtakes us. Quinn's small smirk fills my heart to the brim and fills me with safety. During the day, we talk of the forest, the strange ways of the world, and the mysteries of the sky. Our fingers brush past each other, tempted to touch yet refusing to be the first to cave in. At night, silence is our refuge, needing no words to fill the space between us. Enough refuge to cling to in my sleep. It is his smile keeping me moving the next day.

Until, that is, I wake to the smell of the staleness of the air around our fire and a tingle in my veins. The jungle sits too still. Too quiet. In that moment before wake fully takes over, my heartbeat talks to me. Ba bum. Ba bum. Ba bum. The fear of death hammers through each beat.

Slipping out of my covers, I crawl on my hands and knees to Quinn. My lips brush next to his ear, fear overpowering my excitement at his closeness. "Quinn," I whisper. "It's a puma!"

His eyes pop open upon hearing the alarm in my words. His arms brush against me, and he crawls through the camp to wake the others. He is stealthy in his movements, practiced like a hundred times over, sure as a hunter starving in the dusk.

My eyes stumble over the west cover of the trees. Yellow eyes transform my fear into a need for survival. Whether it is his survival or mine, I am still not sure.

Quinn finds his pack and pulls a pistol from its side pocket. He is silent as he moves. But not quite silent enough.

It's the click of the safety that alerts the animal, just as the other three men make a move for their own weapons. They squat on the ground and brace themselves like monkeys.

I am left singled out, alone in the cover of a fire long burnt out. I shuffle backwards and take refuge behind the four men bordering the tree line.

The puma tracks them as they circle, bodies rotating as they point their guns.

Smart enough to use the trees for cover, the puma ignores them all, his eyes locked only on his prey: me.

One footstep at a time, I step backwards to the safety of one of the largest trees around. I grasp for a handhold and struggle to breathe. In. Out. In. Out.

When I was young, I watched the fangs of a puma clench the flesh of children in the forest. I had wandered too far from home and watched as the village children played in the forest. I remember my envy for them, my desire to share in their games and laughter. I also remember how quickly my desire changed to fear and sorrow. I had been the only one saved. For my misbehavior, I was punished with confinement for a month. A month of dreams covered in the stench of rotting flesh and bloodied cloaks.

Transfixed by my childhood memory, I forget my surroundings and neglect to notice the puma's increasing proximity. The puma's tan skin stretches out as its fangs drool for my flesh. More than one hundred pounds of pure fury lash out with the force of a thunder cloud just as I turn. The soles of my feet reach deep into the crevasse of each nook the tree has to offer. I climb faster than I breathe. Seven feet up, my boots slip on the growth of the bark, and I lose my grip. I fall, dangling from my fingertips as the claws of the beast reach the tree. My calves burn with agony when the puma's claws dig into my skin. It yanks my feet closer to its grasp as I scream.

Gunfire rings out, one from each man. One shot for each beat of my heart. The echo of the shots is deafening in my ears.

Two pairs of hands reach for me and pull me down from the tree.

"You okay? Natalia, are you okay?"

I don't know whose words they are, for I am far too distracted by the terrified look in Quinn's eyes. Several feet away, his stance holds strong, pistol still hot in his hands. It is not the dead animal his eyes fall to. It is not my eyes he looks upon either, but that of my ripped britches. My jeans and skirt are soaked with blood. My bare skin lies exposed above the ties of my laces. The thrashed stripes in my skin drench the socks on my feet.

"Why is your blood blue?" he whispers.

The others freeze at his question. Their eyes drop to my legs, mesmerized by what they see. They forget they are helping me down, and I forget the pain overtaking my legs.

I don't take my eyes off Quinn, refusing to let fear overtake me once more. I study the movement of his eyes, the arch of his brows, and the small tilt of his head. Confused at his words, I find the mark his stare holds. The intake of my breath pains me, razor sharp and paralyzing. "I don't know."

My voice shakes as I drop to the ground, nearly falling into the giant cat's grasp once more. Even dead, the giant beast nearly paralyses me. As I pull myself up, the others wrench their hands off me, apprehensive as they scrunch their eyes. "I don't know!" The blood pours from my shins as I struggle to put weight on my feet.

They stand there in silence and stare at the shimmer of blue mixing with the red oil of my blood.

Mr. Bailey breaks the stunned silence and grabs my hands. "It's okay. I'm sure it's nothing. We need to focus on stopping the bleeding."

He picks me up like an infant, cradling me in his arms. He carries me away from the body of the dead puma. Blood drips from my toes as we walk. It stans his pants and soaks into the linen of my dress. He sits me on the bedrolls just as Quinn appears with handfuls of gauze and liquids sure to cause more pain.

I was always told my death would be brief. An immense amount of pain, but short lived. This is what I tell myself as I feel the burn of my leg throb and the sting of my ripped skin yelling wrath at me. If I were to die, it would have happened by now.

"They are deep Natalia, I'm going to need to put in a few stiches," Mr. Bailey says.

Lying back as he begins to work, tears flow down my cheeks. I feel the pressure of his hands on my legs, but the burning of my flesh can't clarify between any other touch or the gashes from the puma. I cry as the wounds are soaked, cleaned, and pricked with a sewing needle. The pain takes over my fear, and the questions dissipate in my head.

I tell myself that this is proof I am no queen. Queens would not fear pain like this. They would embrace it, hold onto it with purpose. They would not cower into the confines of their mind to try and disappear. I would not keep forgetting to breathe. In. Out. In. Out.

Quinn grabs hold of my hand, and Ryan whispers condolences at my side. He brushes the hair out of my face, knowing it is Bailey who is refusing to slow. Darius, at his side, rushes to get him everything he needs before I have time to panic. Panic more than I already am.

"Put pressure on it. Get her something to take for the pain."

Mr. Bailey pushes orders out as I lie numb on the ground. My bedroll is soaked to the touch. He weaves the needle in and out of my skin, but just after his work begins, my mind fades. The children of the forest are dead and I am a child once more. Crying in the protective arms of my father. My tears dull to help me withstand the anguish.

At last, Bailey collapses at my side and takes my hand out of Quinn's. "Please forgive me. Please." My calf holds three stripes of stitched skin. From my ankle, to just under my knee, my flesh is now a patch of knitwork.

The agony in his voice travels straight to my heart, immobilizing my pain and pulling me deeper toward the earth. My limbs become numb, much as they did before sleep overtook me in the darkness of the cave.

"Please forgive me." His voice jumps, scratching with emotion.

"Of course, Mr. Bailey. There is nothing to forgive." I wipe the tears away from my eyes. "Thank you for saving me over and over again."

My senses take in the burning torment on my leg. I smell the flesh burning from the oils and solutions poured onto my skin. I taste the blood in my cheeks where I had chewed to distract from the pain in my leg. I feel the warmth of the bodies hovering over me, each man's face filled with protection. Pity. Fear. My eyes grow heavy as Mr. Bailey helps me swallow more pills for the pain. More water. He offers more and more comforts. I relax at Mr. Bailey's side and drift off to sleep.

It takes me with a force stronger than that of the dragons' magic that I tried so hard to keep at bay. I drift in and out of sleep as the pain tremors beneath my skin. Like vipers, their teeth penetrate me over and over again until long at last, the venom takes over and numbness becomes my solitude.

I dream of the dragon keeping me hidden from the world. But unlike when I was awake, this keeper streaks the world with fire. He plummets to the ground over the mountain's fiery pits. His wings soar out like waves, crashing into the sky like a tsunami. His anger emanates from his jaws as I watch my tiny trunk of belongings turning to ash in his path.

I see myself walk from the cave, over the lava-torn earth with fire raging under my feet. My hands reach up to the darkened sky, my eyes itching from the smoke of the earth. The dragon soars toward me, crashing to the ground at my feet, his talons grasping at my neck as he falls. His eyes close as death takes him. I bend down to him, taking hold of my necklace in his grasp.

I grab for my necklace as I wake, the sun already mid sky, and the light coming in through the leaves of the trees.

"We need to head back." Mr. Bailey paces in front of the fire pit. "She can't walk on that. She needs to give it time to heal."

"No!"

Quinn snaps his head in my direction, startled by my assertiveness.

I push my aching body up to elbows, the sleep cracking from my eyes. "We are close. I know we are." I adjust the blanket on my legs as I move into a sitting position.

"You can't walk, Natalia. This is crazy," Darius says.

"We are closer to Estancia than from where we started." I massage my healthy leg, refusing to look at any of them. "We keep moving forward."

"No dig is worth you going cripple. We need to turn back," Darius says.

"It's not just a dig!" I say. "It's my home. I have to know! I have to find answers! Please!"

"Maybe we can take turns carrying her," Ryan says. "Take more breaks than normal."

"No." I stop what I am doing and look each man in the eye. "I will walk. Give me the rest of the day, maybe the night. By tomorrow I will walk."

"How?" Quinn says. "You needed 28 stitches. A puma nearly tore your leg off." Sauntering toward me, he kneels to meet me head on. "If we keep going, you will let us carry you. You will let us help you."

I meet his glare, hard and unwavering, and nod my promise.

Ryan accepts the new agreement and nudges at the gauze that remains at my side. A pool of blood drains from my bedroll, soaking the dirt. He moves to clean up the mess. He pours the bowl of blue shimmering water into the ground, letting it seep into the dirt, coloring the ground in its wake.

I feel the quake hit in my bones before it finds life in the earth. I don't know why. Or how. And I can't really explain it, but I feel as though it started with me. As if somehow or another, I could have caused it. My insides vibrate against the solidness of the earth and the pain in my leg sours, with its rhythm pulsating even faster.

The ground rumbles and quakes, and the earth splits at the site of my spilled blood. It cracks its way through the woods, a thunderous moan forcing its way up to the mountains in the West. It wakes the mountain in their path forcing the mountain to breathe out its first breath. The ground shakes ferociously.

We brace the ground with our hands and wait the quake out. A cloak of dust settles on the ground, shifting the earth back into place.

Dirt enters my skin at the tips of my nails. The mustiness of the jungle overcomes me, and I have difficulty resuming the conversation where it left off. "The mountain has woken," I whisper. "I think it was my fault."

"What does that mean?" Mr. Bailey says.

"Earthquakes signal the rise of a volcano."

"And coincidentally it started as your blood poured into the earth?" Darius says. "I'm not buying it."

"Regardless of whether you buy it or not, it happened. We need to be more careful from here on out," Mr. Bailey says. "Things are obviously happening that are well beyond our grasp. Does anyone else know about your blood, Natalia? Did they ever take your blood at the hospital? Or the institute?"

Confusion sweeps over my face. "Why would they take my blood?"

"That's how people check for illness. To see if you're healthy. That sort of thing."

"They thought she was crazy, Pops, not sick, remember?" Quinn says.

"Can you see crazy in someone's blood?" I say.

Mr. Bailey smiles at me. "Only if it were blue."

My voice smiles back. "But you do not think I am crazy."

"No, no, I definitely do not."

Darius stalks over the broken ground and pulls various supplies out of his pack. He begins to skin the giant cat as he talks. "Do you know why it would be blue?"

But it is hard to concentrate. The smell and sounds of Darius's work cloud my thoughts. The rip and tears of the animal's flesh penetrates my skull. The smell of its meat is the first remembrance of unease I have had since waking in the dark.

I remain silent regarding the question at first. Debating. Pondering my truth from the truth the world might hold. "The dragon scales I ate were blue. They were the magic that held me in my slumber."

Darius drops his skinning knife to the ground. They all stare at me speechless, wonder and awe clear in their eyes.

"You got any more?" Quinn says.

I grin despite myself. "No, I believe I'm fresh out."

"Pity," he says. "One of those would come in handy if the old man here ever forced me back to school."

"I thought you wanted to go to school," Ryan says.

"When we are done here, kid, when we find Estancia, you might be able to buy your own damn school," Mr. Bailey says.

"Did you ever go to school, Natalia?" Ryan says.

"Privately." My thoughts reach into my past. "I had a variety of tutors, all whom worked with me privately."

Quinn sits at my side, his neck bent, fidgeting with his hands "Tell us your story, Natalia." They ignore their fallen belongings from the quake. They ignore the mess Darius is making out of the cat's hide, and they watch me. Nervous, maybe, but with sanity in their eyes. Even after my blood spilled, even after an admission of my dragon scales, I know these men do not think I am crazy. They didn't when we first met and they certainly do not now as they follow me through the forest. They were forfeiting their safety to accompany me on this journey. Men who have done nothing but protect me, care for me, and trust me.

The three eldest follow Quinn's lead and sit. Forming a circle around me, they put aside their earlier tasks and wait to hear my tale. Even Darius leaves the hide.

I flash my eyes around the circle but try to keep my thoughts straight. Where do I even begin? How do I even explain the depths of my past? Will they think differently of me? Will their reason for following me change into that of skepticism?

"There was a prophecy of my death." I look to the sun for clarity. Through the thickness of the trees around me, beams of light shine off the men. Bouncing from the greenery to the ash of the fire, the light glimmers off the remains of the blue at my feet.

"I was to save the Kinodans."

I pause to adjust the gauze on my leg. The blood no longer seeping through.

My voice quivers. "I was born at Kinoda, you see, during a time of great turmoil, when the mountain flamed and warriors lost their lives to the forest. My mother was sacrificed on the alter during my birth."

I take a deep breath, determined to gain the courage to go on and resist the tremble in my thoughts. "It would have been a great honor to be my mother.

"At six, the new emperor of Kinoda chose me to be a gift to the King of Iritan. I remember being lined up and beautified with all the other girls from my village. Our hair was brushed and new dresses hung over our shoulders. It was the very first time I had ever worn shoes." I feel my cheeks flush at the memory, then feel the color fade as quickly as it appeared. "One of us was to be chosen for the king, the others chosen for the mountain.

"He took a liking to me, that king. I'm not sure why. I don't recall doing anything different than all the other girls. So I was taken to be raised in solitude, free from impurifications."

I stop to pull my shoulders back, and a small smile forms at the rim of my lips. "My father was gifted gold in payment for his future sacrifice. For *my* future sacrifice. Once I came of age, I was to marry the king and breed him two sons. At the birth of my second son, I would receive the same fate as my mother. My death would provide immortality to the king's bloodlines, while also protecting his people from perishing. The spill of my blood would drip on each soldier to protect them from conquest. Because of me, Kinoda and Iritan would be united."

Fierce grief overcomes me and I struggle to my feet, my weight favoring my good leg. The four men stand in response to my assertiveness.

Turning my back on them, I whisper to the edge of the forest. "The night of my first bleed, I was taken from my bed and pulled from my rooms. I was buried in darkness that now lingers inside me. Darkness I fear will always linger in me." Turning to face them, I raise my voice. "And I woke to discover all my people dead. Long dead. A civilization wiped clean, barely finding a page in the history books that your beloved schools teach."

Everyone. Every single person I ever knew. Dead. I drop to my knees and hot tears wind their way down my face. "I failed them. Each and every one of them, I failed."

"Natalia." Quinn moves closer, but his words are cut off with my cries.

Anguish pushes out of my gut and vibrates off the tree lines. "They are all dead. And I should have stopped it!" I grind my fists against my eyes. "I should have been allowed to stop it…I just…I want…." My voice drops once more. So much so that the men at my side drop to their knees to hear me finish. "I just want to know why. Why wasn't I allowed to save them?"

Chapter Seventeen
Quinn

The clouds roll in at dusk. They hold a fate to bright to ignore and force a layer of fog onto the ground that blankets their campsite. The furious clouds push past the wind as it howls and brings in a thunder as fierce as a thousand volcanos. They turn from grey to black in a matter of minutes, screaming a warning to anyone in their path. The safest course would be to escape ahead of the storm. But none of them refuse to turn away.

"We need to move to higher ground. Now." The urgency in Bailey's voice is clear and no one pauses to consider his implications. They need to get away from the thickest growth of the forest and the dips in the ravine that could drown them in seconds. "Get the tents up! Get them up now!"

The men pull down the tents as Natalia dumps everything in sight into the nearest of their bags. It is not a tight or efficient pack up, but it doesn't need to be. It just needs to be enough to save them from the terror a jungle storm can offer. One tree hit by lightning. All it takes is one to fall before the rest around them crumble like dominoes.

The humidity cools as the storm approaches. Minute by minute their time runs shorter. Even before a storm, the heat leaves

Quinn's clothes wet to the touch. Now, it drips with a mixture of sweat and spits of rain.

With just a few more zips and ties to go, the dark clouds open up, and the ocean falls out upon them. Too frantic to scream, they pull their packs on their backs and begin a laborious trudge to higher ground, except for Natalia, who cannot yet walk. Ryan pulls the packs off her back as she is placed on Quinn's back with the swiftness mirroring that of the storm. Her legs wrap around his waist, as her arms tangle around his neck. Darius takes Quinn's other bags and they begin to slog once more through the forest.

But it will not be a storm they can escape. In the thick of the jungle, there is never truly anywhere to go. There is no nearby village. Not a bungalow or empty field. There is nowhere. Water pours down their faces as they let the forest floor crash mud onto their pant legs. The trees groan as their limbs are thrashed from side to side.

Bailey batters at the front of the path with a machete. Quinn and Natalia follow behind. Pushing as mush foliage out of the way as possible, they hope the path remains clear for Darius and Ryan in the trail left behind.

Lightning cracks in the sky, penetrating the air around them with a pulsation bright enough to illuminate the jungle around them. It forks in the sky like Poseidon's trident and curses everything in its path. But it also holds light and a brief rhythm that adds a tint of music to the wind. A simple dance of clarity. One hundred feet to the East holds a clearing. It screams to become their refuge.

Without the time or aridity to set up a tent, Ryan and Darius tie two sets off ropes around the nearest trees. The tent's plastic is tied between the ropes, and a hammock emerges between the barks of both trees. Quinn steadies Natalia into the safety of its protection and pauses as she unwraps her weight off his back. He pauses, just long enough to ensure it holds her weight, and he scurries off to help his companions.

Three more hammocks are up in a matter of minutes. They hang as a square among the trees, solidifying into divans swaying with the wind. The last of the five tents is strung higher up into the trees, providing a roof for the floating shelters. The darkness of the sky does not foretell how long the storm plans on staying. Staying off the ground keeps them safe from not only the drifting waters but also from the forest life that will not stay away without the protection of a fire.

Bailey, Ryan, and Darius all take turns securing their packs in the branches of the trees while Quinn tests the weight of Natalia's hammock once more. When he is sure it will hold, he climbs in next to her and wipes the water off his face with the sleeve of his shirt. She has a new bandage already wrapped around her leg.

Their shoulders push against each other as the hammock cradles them in and their feet hang down to the forest floor. Resting just above the foliage of the ground, their feet swing with the wind. Quinn adjusts his weight tentatively and moves to lay with his head in the opposite direction of Natalia. They let their weight relax with the gravity of the hammock and take in the sound of the rain pounding on the ground. With their weight evenly distributed, he allows himself a moment to calm his thoughts.

"Are you okay?" Quinn says.

"Yes. But this is definitely something else new to me." She, too, wipes the water out of her face. "Not the storm, of course, but being out in it. It's invigorating!"

"Invigorating?" He says. "Maybe you are crazy!" He smiles as he tries to hide his laugh.

"I'm serious!" She says. "The way we fought was like that of war! The way you moved and planned and did it all while in the thicket of the rain pouring so hard we could barely hear two feet in front of us! The noise alone echoes off the ground like drumbeats!"

"That's what we call panic," he says. He pulls a blanket out of the nearest pack and hands it to Natalia. Taking one for himself as well, he dries the water of the bare surfaces of his skin. He runs it through the thickness of his hair like a towel.

"It makes me feel alive," she laughs, as she too begins to dry herself off.

Chapter Eighteen
Natalia

Truth be told, I like being off the ground at night. The swinging beds keep us a perfect distance from the ground while also close enough to each other to keep a roof over our heads with the extra tent. I also like being able to share one with Quinn. Gravity nestles our bodies together side by side. His warmth helps dry my clothes from the rain. His tender touch of my injured leg reassures me that the wound will heal.

The forest floor becomes alive at night with all things that crawl and creep and sometimes even sting. The ants become waves of an ocean current, always moving as one. Spiders as big as your fist will sneak into each current, sometimes becoming one with the floor itself. Although I was never raised to fear such things, it is something that is preferable to be away from. The campfire always kept such creatures an arm's length at bay, but now, it is a concern distant in my memory.

Instead of fear, I was taught acceptance. Maybe even a little reverence. Whether it be with the long sleeves to keep the bugs away or maybe even a shawl, the heat has always been more dangerous than the life of the forest floor. This, too, was always something I was just made aware of. It is a part of the circle of life. It is what helps create the heartbeat of the jungle.

It is, however, quite amusing to see Ryan squirm from the spiders and Darius prance away from the snakes. Quinn swats at the mosquitos and ducks his head with the monkeys following us from overhead. And Mr. Bailey is always there to soothe away their fears. He is a master at tricking the small beasts into traveling another direction. He often manages to find a way around them entirely. He, too, feels the heartbeat of the jungle and knows how to coax it to safety.

"Natalia, are you still awake?" Quinn's voice is barely a whisper over the rain pattering down around us.

"Of course."

"Would you really have married him?" Quinn says. "A king three times your age?"

"Yes." I don't even pause to consider my answer. "It would have been an honor."

"Even if you didn't love him?"

"Love has nothing to do with marriage."

"Love has everything to do with marriage." He leans up on his elbows to get a better look at me. "It is what you strive for. It is what I hope to strive for. When your heart becomes so in sync with another person that you couldn't imaging spending your life without them. When they are all you think about. For the rest of your life. It's their safety. Their happiness." He relaxes his weight back into the hammock. "Shouldn't that be what a marriage is based on?"

"You speak of the love a child holds for a parent. Or a leader for their people. Of course, there is love."

"But there is also love with passion. Being in love is very different then loving a parent."

"Have you always talked in riddles? Or is it just when I am around?" I say.

"Maybe love was the true reason you were secluded and kept in isolation as a child. Or maybe just because of passion. Your king didn't want you to know such a thing existed."

"Tell me about it then, Quinn. Teach me the difference between loving someone and being in love with someone."

"I have never been in love, Natalia. I'm sure my explanation wouldn't do it justice."

"Try," I say.

"Well… I imagine it is a feeling that starts on your skin. Almost like it was going to melt off if it were not touched. Then it probably goes to the butterflies in your stomach. An eagerness that won't go away. I'm sure it hits the heart, pulsating so fast you feel like you can't breathe. It's a hunger. A desire that is based on emotions. Trust. Care. Concern. Pleasure."

"For never being in love it sounds like you know an awful lot about it."

Quinn's gaze moves to a sleeping Mr. Bailey. "My parents were in love."

"Maybe I would have loved the king."

His eyebrows raise at me as he tries to suppress a laugh. "Maybe over time you could have. But isn't that part of the problem? You were never promised time?" Silence envelopes us as I consider the facts of his question. Because he is right. I was never meant to live a long life. I was never meant time. I was never meant to love. "With all my heart, I hope you find it one day, Natalia. I hope love is the second chance that you have been given. And I hope with all my heart that it is with someone who deserves it."

Chapter Nineteen
Quinn

They leave the next day at sunrise. Natalia barely limps.

If it were him attacked by a blood thirsty feline, not even God Almighty could convince him to keep going. A limp would at least give reason for her to lean on him, to brush against his shoulders, or allow him to carry her in his arms. But here she is, walking as if she merely had a sprained ankle.

He treks through the thick, animal-infested jungle, and keeps lookout behind her, just in case. He wants nothing more than to protect her. To save her from the next savage beast or prevent her from the unknown mysteries that may wait ahead. He wants to stop her tears. He wants to help her find all the answers to her questions.

But emperors and kings? Girls thrown into mountains? Sacrificed on an altar? Kidnapped from her bed? There is no philosophy class in the world that could have prepared him for this. Her sad story made him want to blubber like a baby, and it wasn't even his life she was talking about.

There is also the small possibility that she is crazy.

But her anger seems so misplaced. Not angry at the sacrifice of her mother. Not the kidnapping or forced death-like sleep that came straight out of a fairy tale. No, she is angry that she wasn't able to carry out her own sacrifice, so angry it nearly immobilizes her.

Yet she journeys on, not knowing how to lace her own boots, refusing to touch the dagger at her side, or fall asleep before anyone else. She finds more comfort in the rescue of the unknown than plumbing and home cooked meals.

Her chin is high. She keeps up, injury and all, and leads the way.

It's funny to him how often he has seen her cry. How often he wants to hold her in his arms knowing that even her worst is better than his best. For even with her tears, he can't imagine holding her strength, her courage.

He didn't get out of bed for a week after his mom died. He learned how to pop jokes and dig an excavation before ever thinking he was strong enough to face his worst fears. And here she is, hiking through the woods looking for them. Seeking her fears as if she is a leopard herself, stalking the prey of truth.

"For the record," he says, "they would all be dead anyway."

Bailey is the only one who stops and turns to him, anger in his eyes.

"It's true! Her sacrifice couldn't have magistified an entire population into eternal life."

"Magistified isn't a word," Darius mutters as he stalks past them both.

"I disagree." He walks past Bailey with a smile in his eyes. "I just magistified Pops here into thinking about the past, and that no matter what we do, the past is the past and we can't change it."

"What if the past affects the future?" Natalia says from several feet ahead.

"Oh, good point." He waves his index finger at Darius. "The girl just magistified me."

"You're a dumbass," Ryan says.

"No actually…." He stops walking and scratches his head. "What kind of dumbass would take into account that every single rubber tree has disappeared? Palm trees and cocoa trees are gone, and we are officially no longer in a freaking rainforest."

Their footsteps falter as they take in their new surroundings. Nothing but chestnuts and vegetation unknown in the deepest parts of this continent grows in their wake. Each tree is covered in the turning colors of autumn.

Natalia attempts to run , but her injured leg forces her to stumble over stumps and rotting logs, and foliage that covers the ground in a thick blanket of color.

Struggling to keep up, Quinn hears the heavy breathing of the men behind them. Reaching the edge of the forest, she stops abruptly. Bending over to catch his breath, Quinn holds his knees so tight he forgets to breathe.

"What the hell?" Pulling himself straight, strong, and curious as the girl in front of him, he no longer needs to remind himself to breathe, for the pure astonishment of their view makes his instincts kick into high gear.

The grove of chestnut trees circles an area of more than fifteen acres. Stones crumble to the ground everywhere the roots meet the lush greenery at their feet. One lone chestnut tree stands in the center of the open circle, easily reaching one hundred feet into the sky.

Her run becomes a slow march.

Quinn follows like a lapdog, uncertain and apprehensive. Roots arch out of the ground like a roller coaster falling off its tracks. His fingers touch the bark, as she clears fallen leaves from the stones circling its base.

"Where are we?" Ryan says from behind.

"Estancia," she whispers. "This used to be Estancia."

Chapter Twenty
Natalia

Be here not made, be here strong.

Grow from the ground, standing above it all.

You shall not falter, you shall not wither.

Shell of the winter, summer, and fall.

Be here not made, be here strong.

You will grow, you will stand.

Dragon breath, fire and ice.

Roots of gilt, fruits of silver.

Be here not made, be here strong.

The song springs from my lips from habit. It is the only thing that stops my cries and screams of weakness. I brought them here only to find desolate growth.

Falling to the ground, I mourn. There is no castle. There is no gold. Not even a villa resembling my old home. Stones crumbled upon more stone. It is all rubble. My entire past. All my hope. Crumbled to the ground.

As Ryan, Darius, and Bailey pull camp, my thoughts are on their excavation tools. Oh, how I wish to excavate my past as much as they. But of course, it is gone. How could I be stupid enough to expect differently? They tried to warn me. With all their tales of the great unknown of Estancia that was never found? Of course, it was gone. It would have been burned to the ground the very first night of my disappearance.

Quinn stays at my side, rubbing my back as I force my chest to rise and fall. My fingers grasp the wood around my neck, the small token of my home now rubble and chestnuts. Nothing but chestnuts.

I wish I knew what happened to my father. To know he was safe when the towers fell around him. To think maybe he found an escape. To imagine him living a long life, growing to an old age, escaping all the sadness and massacres I left behind.

Somehow Quinn knows that his presence is all I need. None of the other men mention it for they, too, understand. His touch on my back is the only thing rooting me to the ground. The only thing assuring me I can do this. I can figure it out. I can remember how to breathe.

Bailey, a man filled with richness in his heart, has barely noticed the lack of treasure. He finds the rubble of rock and stone a treasure of its own, and he smiles to the other men every time he finds two stones still welded together. His giddiness spreads to Ryan and Darius like a common cold. They are men in their glory, with or without the gold.

Before the camp was set up, day break hits, and Bailey drools over a carving left in a rock at the base of a tree. Digging up the six-foot rock, sweat breaks out on his face. He tries his best to hide his smile, but with little luck. Darius and Ryan set up tents, and his only son mourns for the heartsick girl who is beginning to wonder if I am crazy after all.

"Maybe this isn't it," Quinn says.

"No, thank you, but no. Even after all the time gone by, the landscape can't hide itself from me. Nor could a chestnut from my father."

As if the thought jostles something inside me, my chin nods at Bailey and his six-foot rock. Grabbing support from Quinn's hand, I drag him over to his father.

He uses tools with spikes and clothes soaked in a damp liquid to polish the stone at its base. He forces it out of the ground. The gray stone stands as high as the immature trees and sparkles in the sunlight, even as its shadow forms a path back toward the forest.

"What is the carving?" I say. "What is it of?"

"Not a picture. I think some sort of scripture." Bailey wipes his forehead with a cloth and he nods at Darius and Ryan. "I'll have the boys take it back to the university to get it translated… somehow."

"Let me read it."

All of his movements stop as he realizes what I imply. Pouring water over the stone, the markings pop into view like a rainbow after a storm. Five feet up from the ground, they meet me at eye level. I move closer and reach out to brush me fingers along each mark. My mouth moves silently as I read.

"Chestnuts stand above the blood-stained earth."

Every eye in the camp turns to me. My words, an accent reemerging, are soaked with haunting emotion. It is no longer fear that holds me to the ground. Not sadness or pity or even anger. It is resolve. Pure, unrelenting, resolve.

"It was my father." I rest my open palm on the words written in a language ancient and obsolete. "He thought my worth greater than theirs."

"Greater than whose?" Bailey says.

"Everyone."

Chapter Twenty-One
Quinn

They have been at the site for three days when Quinn's thoughts start to eat away at him, digging into his flesh like a disease. Outrage at the horrors she has faced consumes him, with not a single ounce of evidence for any of it. There is no proof of her dragons. Nor of the magic or even an outline of her own home. Aside from the chestnut hanging at her neck, there is no other proof that any of it was actually real.

They have found nothing but marks of destruction. Time did not tear down the walls of her old home, nor did erosion crumble her belongings and memories into dust. Not only was life taken from here, so was all proof of life.

Throwing a branch into the fire, Quinn begins to pace. "There has got to be something here! Something!"

Ryan pauses as he shuffles a spoonful of beans into his mouth. "There are some great finds here. That carving itself can unleash a language no one has ever seen."

"The chestnuts, too," Darius says. "They don't belong here. Put it all together and I can't help but think we are missing something."

Quinn raises an eyebrow. "Like what?"

"Like, for example, what would have happened to Natalia's father after he kidnapped a village sacrifice? Stowed her away and put a dragon in her charge for a few centuries?" Darius says.

Natalia puts her spoon down in the bowl that rests in her lap. "He would have been killed. Along with every single man who had ever worked at his side."

"But where?" Darius pauses to take another spoonful. "This was his home. You said it yourself, you had servants, and a dozen men who helped hide you. When you never showed up to marry the king, someone would have noticed. Someone would have come here looking for you and slaughtered anyone in their path."

"Wreckage lies here, but not a slaughter," Ryan says.

"Which means they were either taken to face the king or went there of their own accord," Natalia says.

"Does that mean we go visit a dead king?" Quinn says.

"That's a choice Natalia needs to make." Bailey motions to her. "But I think we are all overlooking an even stronger possibility." He stands to poke the fire. "The treasure of Estancia."

"It's not here, Pops," Quinn says.

"I think it is." He slides the stick into the blazing fire in front of them. The smell of smoke fills the air around them and the fire turns blue. "What if Natalia is the treasure? Natalia of Estancia?"

Chapter Twenty-Two
Natalia

I always knew he was gone, but the evidence of it is still overwhelming. I try so hard to remember back to the last time we spoke. The last time we hugged in an embrace or smiled at each other from across the room. Of course, there are plenty of memories I have, just none I can remember as the last. These are where my thoughts lie while everyone sleeps around me in the black of night. Not even the stars shine brightly upon the sky in a night as dreary as this. But the rustle of the fire blazing back to life forces my thoughts to stop. Forcing my eyes to open even wider, I sit up.

Quinn jerks awake and tumbles out of his sleeping bag. His face, still covered in sleep, catches the fire light. Bailey, Ryan, and Darius stand like icicles on a warm winter day.

Surrounded by half a dozen men, two stand apart. One as old as the wood from the fire stares like a crow into my fear-filled eyes. The other works on the fire, ignoring the confusion of the awakening men.

"If you are not the girl with dragon magic in her veins, tell me how it is we found you." The young man continues to build up the fire as he steals glances at me. No one else dares to speak a word. "My name is Cyprien. My grandfather here is Gaeetan, and we are here to strike a bargain with you."

"Look…I don't…." Natalia cuts Bailey off with a simple raise of her palm.

"You come with us, leave your friends behind, and I will lead you to the answers you seek."

I don't answer. Instead, I ponder this man in front of me, a man who followed me into the forest from an unknown land with unknown desires and ambitions. I look at the old crow with wrinkles stuck on his face. I look at the black oils slick in his hair. I consider my true wishes deep in my heart. "No."

I drop the sleeping bag in my grasp. My shoulders pull back and my chin rises. "We already found the answers I seek."

Silence penetrates the camp. The old man picks at the rocks around the fire with his cane. The unknown strangers hold their position on the outskirts of the forest.

"But you still have unfinished promises."

Cyprien's face softens as he hunches over and exhales from his chest. "Natalia…" he whispers. "We know who you are. And I can give you everything you seek." He takes a step closer to me. "There is no need to fear us if you come willingly. But Iritan holds grudges and will never stop hunting you. They will rise again with the spill of your blood."

"Are you Iritan?" I say.

Walking over to Gaeetan, he places a hand on the old man's shoulder. "Gaeetan is the oldest descendent of the empire, with stories passed down through blood, generation after generation. He has been responsible for our people and yearns to pass. He holds truths that no other can hold. Truths about you, Natalia." Dropping his hand from the old man, he approaches me. He takes my hand into his, and a tenderness sings to my blood.

I am not sure why I distrust him so. Perhaps the blue in his hair or the lies in his eyes. Maybe it is the truth his words hold or the old crow always at his side. The wrinkled old man reminds me of the moment when a six-year-old girl trembled at the chance to matter. He reminds me of a very old king.

Quinn is quick to step forward, but Darius places his hand on his chest and stops him in place. He gives Quinn the strength he needs to remain rooted in place.

"Is he in charge?" Bailey says.

Cyprien keeps his eyes locked on me. "Yes, but I am to be his successor. You can help our people rise again, Natalia. Come with me and we can both bring the empire back."

Quinn pushes Darius's hand out of the way and moves closer to the two. "She is not coming with you." His clenched fists are clear for all to see.

"The prophecy needs to be fulfilled," Gaeetan says.

"We will find another way. Prolong the prophecy. Perhaps even create a new empire. A greater one. We can do it together. We can overcome this." Cyprien talks to me with a calmness that settles over the camp. His demeanor is not only alluring but also quietly demanding.

"Her father couldn't let her marry with the intent of a sacrificed death. His obedience did not lie with Iritan. Nor should hers," Bailey says.

"Where does your obedience lie, Natalia? With the kingdom and future of your people? Or hiding among the ashes of the depraved dragon fliers?"

A small smile creeps onto my face as I shake away Cyprien's fingers.

His blue-tipped hair falls in his eyes, astonished as I look down at my fingers in distaste.

"The dragons. My obedience lies with the dragons."

His eyes turn cold.

The wind blows restlessly as Gaeetan approaches, a force awakening as he lumbers toward the fire. "You will die, girl! This life is not yours to hold!" His scream echoes off the surrounding woods. "It is too late for you! The mountain already woke, forfeiting all hope you ever had!"

Silence penetrates the small camp once more, a silence so deep only the fierce beat of my heart is heard. Little does he know it was me who woke the mountain in the first place. Accident or not, I will not sub come to his idle threats.

Gaeetan throws his cane in the fire and the blaze roars to life. "You wait and see girl. You wait and see!" He stalks off, hovering in the darkness of the forest.

"Forgive me," Cyprien whispers at the coldness across her face. "Truly." He turns to leave, his men following behind.

They leave with no other words, no other warnings or intents.

The five of them hold their stance well into the waking day, refusing to move until they are certain the intruders are gone, far from earshot.

"Who are the dragon fliers?" Ryan says.

I sit down on my sleeping bag and tug at the bandage around my calf. "Anyone who believes in dragons. Prior to … *everything* … I always thought them a myth. Evidently, my father was a flier."

"People hold dragon myths all over the world. If we search them out, the ones in the area, maybe they can help us," Bailey says.

"No." Natalia takes the remainder of her bandages off and reveals skin smooth and flawless. "Fliers can't help us. We need to find the dragons."

Chapter Twenty-Three
Quinn

After cleaning up camp, they trek back to the villa before planning a path forward. Now, knowing the true location of Estancia, there is nothing stopping them from returning.

Darius struggles with the decision the most. He pouts and scours the landscape with his eyes, as if etching it into his memory. He takes pictures of every relic, every angle of every stone, and every carving they find.

Ryan and Bailey bustle about like chipmunks. They ponder the histories of dragons and have a hundred different ideas of where they might find them. They deliberate which valleys would hold the most potential, which mountains the strongest likelihood.

If Natalia's father found a dragon, with all the pictures she sketched the first few days out, it's possible they exist, but he can't grasp how to prove it.

He feels Darius's doubts and listens to Ryan's arguments. They both think Natalia needs to lie low, hide out until the pompous king forgets about her and moves onto something less tainted by resurrected prophecies. He is not so sure. She hid out for centuries. How much more hiding could she possible endure? Maybe she is right. Maybe she needs to find the dragons and end the prophecy once and for all. But then again, wasn't it a dragon that put her to sleep for eight hundred years?

"We need to regroup at the villa and discover the local dragon myths," Natalia says.

Quinn stays at the tail end of the group as they hike through the forest the same way they came. He climbs over decayed and fallen trees and trips over branches lying hidden under the false illusion of a successful dig, all maintained on a single camera lens. Because, per Bailey's arguments, they can't carry history back by sled.

Natalia hikes through the jungle and floats through the thick brush as if wings have sprouted out of her back. But with each elegant step she takes, more unease falls over him. She has lost her home, nearly lost a leg, and has been followed into the jungle by a strange group of men. Yet, her stance is straighter. Her posture taller and full of pride. She no longer trips or favors her injured leg. Instead, her eyes watch the sun's path.

One day when the wind blows soft, she slows and falls back to his side.

She raises an eyebrow. "Why do you pull away?"

"An entire group of people want you dead," Quinn says. "I think that is reason enough to feel restless."

She gives him a long look, her gaze dim. "Yes, I suppose it is."

Quinn touches her shoulder for balance as they climb over the remains of a hollow log. He goes rigid at the heat of her flesh. Anxiety twists in his stomach.

She pauses, turning her body parallel to his. She gives him a modest smile and lets her words crash into him. "The future is unknown. Even if it will rain fire. You forget that I have always been destined to die. This is nothing new."

He laughs weakly. "What? What on earth would make you think a statement like that would help me feel better?"

Her fierce eyes fill with determination and resolve. "I cannot say, but I feel something stirring. I can't explain it, I just know we are scratching the surface. They knew who I was in the town square before ever speaking a word to me. They knew to find me in Estancia. Then. And now. Even the dragon came at that time for a reason. I just need to find out why."

"I think you already know why."

"And why is that, Quinn?"

"Because your father didn't want you dead, and neither did fate." He stares at her. "Do you ever wonder why you woke when you did?"

"Every day," she says. "Every single day."

"Do you ever wonder if maybe it was not to sacrifice your life to a bunch of old showoffs, but maybe to live life here with someone standing beside you?"

"I was never allowed to wonder such things before, Quinn. It's hard for me."

"Yet you did not leave with them in the square, and you would not leave with them when they came for you in Estancia." His eyes search the sky. "You fear them, Natalia, just as much as you fear failure. Maybe it's time to accept it?"

She doesn't answer. Instead, her lips tighten and she shakes her head. "I have never known choices of my own. They have always affected others. Even hundreds of years later, my life holds consequences to those who are in it—to a group of people refusing to go extinct and even to you. My choices even affect you." She takes a long, slow breath. "For the first time in my life, I am trying to think of me first. Before everyone and everything else. Before I

115

make any more choices, I want to see the options. Can you please help me with that?"

He bites his lip, trying to see everything through her eyes, to live a second with the weight she holds on her shoulders. He nods his head.

They catch up to the group. Aside from the occasional snake or grumpy tamarin, they push through the remainder of the jungle without trouble. Darius kills rodents, letting Ryan cook them for dinner. Bailey takes the first watch at night, until Quinn nudges him and takes his spot to watch into the darkness and listen to the stir of the night.

Natalia is deathly quiet at night and that affects the men. Ryan moves his cot closer to watch over her each night, staying awake with Quinn until at last she falls asleep.

Quinn tries to convince her to use a tent, but she insists that the stars are all the cover she needs. They follow suit and find the shadows of the forest their blanket, covering them through the thickest of night.

Days pass before they reach the Jeep and the edge of the never-ending jungle. Mud covers their faces, and their backs ache with the trials of adventure. They slouch into the vehicle, and the engine roars to life as if a warning.

The drive across the barren land on dirt roads seems to take longer than the trip through the jungle, as their muscles fight back and their thoughts roam free.

Bailey stops the car before pulling into the villa's driveway and reaches for the gun at his side.

The front door is open and swinging back and forth from the breeze in the humid day. One by one they climb out of the car, urging Natalia to stay put. But her eyes plead with Quinn, and he can't insist she is safer by herself. Grasping her hand, he keeps her body shielded behind his. He is one more piece of armor, to one more unknown danger.

They find the villa ransacked, drawers thrown askew, furniture flipped and torn to pieces. Glass and china are shattered across the tile floor.

Santino hangs by a rope secured around his neck at the main entryway of the house. His blue face tells of a struggle long gone from his limbs. His sandals lie on the floor three feet under his blue toes. He is a statement, written clearly in front of the staircase.

Quinn drops to his knees. His hands cover his mouth, too shocked to speak, too overcome to move. Since the moment he found Natalia in the darkness of the cave, he felt momentum. An urge to continue moving forward. Now, there is nothing but the immobilizing fear seeping into his heart.

The world stills as they stare at the poor dead man.

Without a word, Darius and Ryan hustle to get the body down, to preserve any dignity the man's soul may hold.

Resentment and frustration bubble inside Quinn, and thoughts of Natalia course through him. Natalia. Poor sweet Natalia. His face turns to her with panic creased into his brows. She stands in the frame of the front door, her face white. Her mouth hangs open while her eyes hold in a thousand tears too shocked to pour out. Her silence echo's more than the death hanging from their ceiling.

Bailey rushes to her, taking her hand in his grasp. He ushers her outside, away from her dead friend. Away from the devastation and the fear of the murderous threat.

The body lies on the floor in front of Quinn. In front of a pair of steps, the dead man will never climb. A blanket from the sofa lies across his face.

"This is madness," Quinn whispers. "What do we do?" His eyes search out Ryan's, then Darius's. He holds no answers. None of them do.

Chapter Twenty-Four
Natalia

Death is an abstract idea, a simple moment in time that cannot actually be seen. A statement of life. It is untouchable. It is the impression of death that was always meant to matter. When a mother dies giving birth to the child, or when a man is killed in war protecting his village, they are making the greatest sacrifice of all, ending one life for another. I was meant for that sacrifice. Never was someone supposed to make it for me. But that is exactly what happened. Santino died because of me.

After the Argentinian police take the body, we sit in the living room. The windows are already boarded up and the glass swept off the floor. The furniture is put back in place. Tea boils on the stove.

My insides rumble and all the strength of certainty is stripped from me. I have seen men dead before. War had struck close to my home many times. Soldiers left and never returned. But they all went willingly. Knowing what their failure in combat might cost them, they still chose to go. But this?

A new fear builds inside me, wobbling like that of a stone at the edge of a cliff. I had always known my fate. Never questioned it. But now ... thinking of that first moment in front of the dragon I was using my strength as a crutch when I should have been balancing on my fear. Fear for my friends, my family. The first dragon scale was likely touching my tongue at the moment my father was facing the same fate as Santino. Probably a death much worse.

Santino's death from friendship must have held a much easier demise than deceit and traitorous acts of defiance like my father's. How selfish of me to never see it. To never cry over my dead father. To never worry over my trusted relationship with Santino or worry for my friends when I refused to leave with Iritan. Every moment with me, every meal and every adventure, I will always be a danger to them.

That is when I see it. A crumpled paper is stuck in the door jamb. I pull the tattered note from its hiding place and, sitting on the floor, I unfold it. Tears pool in my eyes, then flow down my cheeks as I read the Anaxcian script.

Bailey finds a place at my side, nestling me in the nook of his arms and reads the scribbled note.

Heed warning my dear girl. Keep the dragon scale close for protection. I found it in your trunks on your first arrival. Please forgive me for at the time I did not know. May the magic that lies within help you create your own destiny.

Santino

My breath holds heavy in my chest, as the others look to me, and I whisper the translation.

"A dragon scale?" Bailey says.

"They must have taken it," Ryan whispers.

"Natalia?"

Darius's voice is raspy. Bending on a knee in front of me, his eyes avoid Bailey's gaze. "I need to plead for your forgiveness." He takes my hands in both of his, cradling them like a shield from the rain in my heart. "I cannot do this. I was not built for it. Bones and crypts sure. But for those who lived long, long ago." He shakes his head.

Fear creeps through my body and I shake at the grasp of my fingertips.

Bailey tries to interrupt. "Darius...."

Darius's eyes plead with me. "I can't do this. I can't stay knowing everything you know. But you can come with me. I can get you on a plane. I can get you to the States. I know people who can keep you hidden, give you a new life."

Ryan jumps to his feet, and Quinn quickly stands behind him. "Darius what the hell are you talking about?"

Darius begs. "Please, Natalia."

His pleas speak to me while placing a shadow on my heart. "I thank you for your service to me, Darius. I cannot make you stay. But I must not leave either. I fear death follows me, and it is my time to face it head-on. For my people and for Santino."

Bailey stands, his voice deep and stiff. "No one is leaving, and no one is facing any more death."

I pull my hands from Darius's grasp and rise from the floor. Standing, with both feet firm on the floor, I shift my regard to Bailey. "Mr. Bailey, I need to find the men who did this."

"That is what the police are for," Bailey says.

"I need to go." I run my palms down the sides of my skirt. "And this time I go alone."

Panic crosses Bailey's face as he shouts, "I promised I would look after you! I can't do that if you go running off!" He turns and glares at Darius. "That goes for both of you."

Bailey's words remain lost within Quinn's sheepish stare. "You are both being ridiculous. Leaving is not an option for *us*, — for any of us." Quinn bites his nails as he stares at his feet. "We stick to the original plan. We look for the dragons."

Darius's face is grim, and I see his resolve crumble in front of him. Broken. Pained. Tormented.

"I fear there is no more time," I say.

"What about the dragon scale?" Quinn says. "We can find where Santino left it. We can use it to save you. Together!"

My eyes flash to his, hot and filled with longing. "Dragon scales cannot save me, only prolong the inevitable."

Bailey approaches me, sadness tugging at the corners of his lips. "No, Natalia. No."

My mask of fortitude slips at his words, and my eyes water. The moisture threatens to spill at any movement. "Please…." I murmur. "There can't be any more on my account. I can't bear it."

The tears fall down my cheeks. The quake in my voice tears at every man in the room. I see it in their slanted eyes. I feel it in the heat radiating from their skin.

Bailey rushes to me. Picking me up in his arms, he cradles me, just as my father had. My arms wrap around his neck as his arms offer protection. My head nestles at the crook of his neck.

He lets me cry. He lets me soak his shirt with my fears.

I breathe him in. The father he is, the father he resembles. Letting the pain in my chest heave, I pour out my sadness for Santino. For Darius. For everything I lost. For everything else I fear I will lose.

He holds me until my tears dry. Grown men are silenced by my grief. I slip from his grasp as though my will and strength were shattered.

"We will discuss it more in the morning. We've had a long day. I must lie down and rest," I say. Although a conversation in the morning would be one person too short, I am glad for Darius. I am glad he had the courage to say what I assume everyone else is thinking. This is not their fight, and it should not be their reason to pass on. If Darius hadn't suggested they stop, perhaps it should have been me.

My father's diversion failed. It was time for me to face my fate.

Chapter Twenty-Five
Quinn

Quinn is pulling the covers down on his mattress when he hears the light knock on the door. Her small frame hovers in the doorway, unsure and apprehensive. Her silk night gown clings to her skin, and her hair falls around her shoulders, curling in waves around her face.

Her sensuous curves beneath the thin layer of fabric fill him with longing, much as it had the first moment he saw her. Without waiting for a response, she steps into the room and softly closes the door behind her.

Quinn gazes at her, acutely aware of his pajama pants hanging low on his hips. A lone t-shirt sits out of his reach, thrown hastily on the middle of his bed. Natalia's bare feet cross the length of his room. She climbs on the mattress in front of him and sits with her eyes burning into him. Crossing her legs, she takes his shirt and hands it to him.

He puts on his shirt and sits down opposite her with his back resting against the headboard. He thinks of the way she holds his gaze, how her eyes linger on his lips. His heart holds desire for her, desires too strong to hold in. Hee can't help but wonder if her desires resemble his own.

She pulls the sheets down and nestles under the covers next to him. She rests her hand on the pillow beside him, and nods slightly as she silently urges him to lie down.

His arms rest under his head as he obliges. Without question, he does as she asks. He comes face to face with her deep brown, honey-filled eyes and her rose-tipped lips. The smell of eucalyptus lies heavy on her skin. His body radiates heat toward the girl who just crawled into his bed.

"I'm glad you found me, you know," she whispers.

"Me too." He smiles and begins to relax at her gentle words. "I can't imagine how much dust would have collected on you if you stayed down there any longer."

A smile finds her eyes, but rests there, never moving to her lips.

She gives him a long look. "You should leave with him. You should leave with Darius."

His mind turns grim, and he takes a deep breath. This is not the conversation he wants to have with her, not his intent with her breath so close to his own. "I'm not leaving you," he says gently. His fingers trace down the length of her shoulder.

"That's what I am afraid of."

Closing her eyes, the silence stretches between them.

His mind races, and his heart pumps faster than a freight train. He brushes his fingers against the arch of her cheek.

Opening her eyes, she takes his hand into hers and squeezes. "I am scared for you, Quinn. I am scared for all of you."

"I thought you said you were trying to think more of yourself?"

Shaking her head at him, she huffs. "You know exactly what I mean."

"And you know damn well I am not going anywhere. We are here for you… I am here for you. So, stop this nonsense and let me be by your side. If it is not what fate wanted, I never would have fallen into that damn cave. And I think you know that."

She smiles at him and nestles down closer to his side. Not another word falls from her lips, but her body relaxes into peace.

Their hands remain clasped as she drifts into sleep. He waits on his own slumber, and the quiet of the room lingers, moving from minutes into hours. He does not want to let go of this moment, nor let it fade into another horror-filled day.

He watches her just as he had that first morning when she allowed sleep to overcome her as dawn found its way over the horizon. He watches the small movements of her eyelids, the rise and fall of her chest, and finally when the night breaks into scattered moments, he drifts off to sleep.

Chapter Twenty-Six
Natalia

There was a moment in the darkness of the dragon's cave when I allowed myself to touch hope. Barely brushing against it, I knew it would be a dangerous thing. I had always known it would be a dangerous thing.

I remember the shine of the scales, the sureness of the dragon's movements. But I can't remember where the hope came from. Did it come from the moment I was pulled from my bed of down, knowing that my fate would soon be aligned with that of my destiny? Or was it when sleep overtook me, freeing me from all my sorrows, all my worries, all the weight that had been laid at my feet. Or was it from the boy? The boy who came to my side, his mouth against mine as he whispered. His movements promised a kiss that would never come. A promise that I still hold on to, and a promise there each time I wake.

The light shone through an opening in the cave, and a boy with marble hair stood up after falling on his face. In my memories, his smile rises from one side and his eyes smile even when he sleeps.

This is what I thinks of as I pretends to sleep: how his hair shades his striking blue eyes, the same now as it had that day so many months ago. For that is now my reason. Not the fallen empire or the dead men hanging in her thoughts, but the beautiful boy in front of me with a pure heart, even when he denies it. He holds the heart of a gentleman who could himself save an empire if that were an option in his path.

Once I am certain he slumbers, I reach up my gown to grasp at the garter secured at my thigh. Peeling away the dragon's scale hidden beneath, I cup open his hand and place the scale in his palm.

I didn't understand at first why the others had not seen the glistening blue behind the crumpled note in the living room's doorframe. But I listened as I felt their hope for finding it and decided they might need to hold onto it more than me. If not for me, then at least for themselves.

They would never let me leave. They would never truly understand. But this is not something that can be stopped. My father may have denied the fulfillment of the prophecy, but it is not something I can hide from any longer. It had only been delayed.

Quinn is what pushes me to want to do more. Be better. His thoughts of me are so high. Now is my time to prove it, to prove my worth to the world.

Slipping out from the warmth of his covers, I silently wish I was born in his time. A time when I could press my lips against his and feel the touch of his abdomen beneath my skin. I wish to steal more than a moment with him. Then, hating myself for my thoughts, wish I could stop such foolish wishes.

Chapter Twenty-Seven
Quinn

She is gone when he wakes, the eucalyptus smell of her skin lingering on his sheets. She not only slipped from his bed in the dark of the night, but she fled the house. Her room is left empty of everything she could carry. The path of her boots leads down the dirt driveway.

Darius, too, had packed up in the night and left only the memory of his presence.

Did they sneak out together, Darius letting her drift in the opposite direction as he scurried back to the States?

"What are you doing?" Bailey says from the top of the stairs.

"Going after her." Quinn mumbles his words as frustration heightens his temper. He slips on his boots and throws his bag toward the door.

"With a parka and boots?" he asks. "Are you nuts?"

"Only for chestnuts," he whispers.

Bailey throws his bag down the stairs, hitting the door frame when it lands. "How much can I pay *you* to stay back?"

"Nothing. Grab my toothbrush, will you?"

"Get your own damn toothbrush," he shouts. "Hey, Ryan! Find my boots, will ya?"

"I'm busy!" Ryan yells from the kitchen. "Where the hell is the kitchen bag? We won't accomplish shit without a damn pot or pan!"

"How much can I pay *you* to stay back?" Bailey shouts as he rustles through the upstairs bathroom.

"Nothing. So grab my toothbrush, too, will you?"

Quinn eases his palm into his back pocket. Cupping the dragon scale in his hand, he feels the pulse of the lizard's blue residue dusting his skin. He secures the scale in his back pocket for safe keeping. "I'm leaving. You're either out in five, or I'm off by myself."

"Who the hell is the parent here?" Bailey says. "Ten! I need at least ten."

Ryan thrusts a map into Quinn's open arms. "I'll help him. You find Kinoda."

"There is no such thing as Kinoda. It doesn't exist anymore."

Bailey pops his head over the railing. "A mountain. They said something about a mountain waking up."

"A volcano? You think Kinoda is a volcano?"

"Check the seismology charts." Ryan pauses halfway up the stairs to look back at Quinn. "If anything woke up, those charts will show us where. That quake the other day, find out its starting point."

Quinn pushes everything off the kitchen table and opens his laptop. Three minutes in, he stumbles across movement from the graphs. A 4.0 on the Richter Scale, directly at the base of a mountain not far from Estancia's path.

"I got it!"

He rushes for the front door. The staircase rumbles as they descend like a herd of elephants stampeding to the jeep. Flustered. Panicked. On a rampage to enter into a world foreign to them, a world that should have died out centuries ago.

"We will find her, Quinn. She couldn't have gotten far." Bailey starts the vehicle but seems to be talking more to himself than Quinn. "We will find her."

Chapter Twenty-Eight
Natalia

I do not need to travel far to pinpoint my destination. A simple walk through the village and someone is tracking me. I am certain of it. I cross the dirt path outside the villa and hope I left long before Darius slipped from the house behind me. He was awake when I left, likely struggling with his decision. If only I could assure him that he was doing the right thing.

Clouds hover in the night sky, and the full moon shimmers off their silver lining. Thunder rolls in the distance. Lightning flashes before my eyes and forces my feet to move a little faster. But I do not acknowledge my fear. My fists clench and I hold on to my will. Queens are not afraid.

I find my way back to the village Quinn took me to a lifetime ago. I see the remnants of stores abandoned for the night and paths once filled with people now deserted. I cross the dragon tiles in the middle of the square while darkness still lingers in the sky. The moon's light shimmers against the scales carved into the cement stones.

The forming storm in the sky threatens to darken out the light, but darkness cannot stop my plans. I was raised to be a queen. And I am not afraid.

Fearful of waking the wrong crowds, I begin to sing softy as my feet move past the village edge.

Come to me, follow me home.

Bring me back to life.

Come to me, help me find my way.

Forever isn't always.

Forever heeds no more.

Come to me, follow me home.

Help me find my way.

Within minutes, half a dozen men follow behind me with swords strapped in their holsters and kerchiefs wrapped around their heads. Their faces hold the same darkness as the blackened sky.

I turn to face them all. I take a breath to fill my lungs and remind myself: in, out. In. Out. With my eyes dry and my solitude firmly hidden, I pull my shoulders back and place her boots on the ground one step at a time. I was groomed for this. Destined for it.

"I'm here for Iritan," I say. "Take me to your prince."

They follow my orders without question.

Nodding to three of the men, the others disappear into the dusk from which they came. There is no question of who I am or why I come at such a late hour. There is nothing at all with these men. Silence follows their every move and envelopes the air around them.

I follow the three men down the paved streets, past the umbrella posts held in store wagons, and along the secluded sidewalks of a sleeping village. They motion to the lone vehicle parked on the town's edge. I climb inside without question.

A short travel in the beaten-up Volkswagen, over bumps and crevasses on a long-forgotten road, and we arrive at a field so large and so open I gasp for air. Never once have I seen so much open space.

The men do not speak to me or soothe my anxiety. Their eyes are cold as they steal glances at me. Their withered movements fill me with distrust. The vehicle that stands at the side of the field looks unlike any I have ever seen, if I even know what it is.

Climbing out of the car, I glimpse the sun peeking over the horizon, the thunderclouds now a memory. I pull courage from the idle light and follow the three men to the craft. I muster the courage to climb inside the aircraft, but apprehension fills my gut. When dragons were born on earth, they flew with the birds, hovering in the skies with their wings spread like the wind. They soared like a current pushing through the sea, then landed on the ground with the elegance of a dancing reptile. But I do not have wings. I was never meant to fly.

Inside the aircraft, I imagine hearing Quinn. He urges me on with each step, and I follow his lead even as I refuse to look at the disappearing ground. You can do this, he says. One step at a time. You can do this.

Chapter Twenty-Nine
Quinn

There is no trace of her. Anywhere. They question everyone they see in the village. "A young girl. Alone. Hair that wraps around your heart like a tendril. Have you seen her?"

Half the day passes before they head to Quinn's volcano. They muster a plan as they travel for three days around the jungle and cross decades-old bridges. There is no room for discussion. It is the quickest route they can consider.

But the travel does not go smoothly. The air conditioning in the car breaks down within the first hour, and the humid air seeps into the car with barely a breeze. They sit in agonized silence.

Bailey drives the entire trip while Ryan studies the map in his hands.

Quinn sits in the back, staring out the open windows at the trees they pass. He watches the villages that hold truths so much like his own. He is crumbling on the inside.

How many of these villages were built from the embers of beautiful young girls thrown into burning ashes, bleeding for the sake of their people? How many of their fathers watched as it happened and pretended to be grateful their family blood was spilled when it was really a curse that followed the land so deep it spread through the ages? A curse indeed.

How many fathers were brave enough to stop it? To have more trust in a fire-breathing dragon than humans? He imagines only one. One man.

Quinn sees only an inkling of what her father must have seen. Of her true worth. Of her true nature. Maybe that was the purpose of her solitude growing up. So others wouldn't see it. So no one else would have the inclination to step in.

Her father had succeeded once, and for some unseen reason the torch was passed to Quinn and his family. His resolve stiffens. May the godforsaken forest be his demise or the tale of the dragon swoop in to swallow him whole. He will save her. From the land – from the people – from herself.

Chapter Thirty
Natalia

We land on a cleared strip in the forest at the edge of the dirt terrain with a castle carved into the side of a mountain. Archways hundreds of feet tall, pillars smoothed to perfection, and carvings encircle the entire side of the mountain. There are carvings of dragons, with their wings spread over the tops of cities, volcanos dripping fire, and people bent to their knees, waiting for a sacrifice that never came. Sandstone chips away at their faces. The ground at their feet lies dark with erosion.

Rocky overhangs and limestone cliffs shadow the castle from the sky where the forest becomes thick once more. The land keeps the castle shaded in the dark and the land gloomy in fog. At the base of the grand castle's entrance is a dirt colosseum meeting the south trail of the airstrip. Hundreds of feet of forest hide daybreak from the ground. Although the thickness of the forest is new to me, this is the architecture I remember from my time.

At the base of the castle's mouth, facing the grand colosseum, a throne sits to one side, bordered by rows of chiseled pews, some made of dirt, others made of stone. Perfectly symmetrical from the east to the west, the seats face the grand entrance to the stone palace. Two pillars corroded by the yellows and browns of time, align with the rays of sunlight sneaking in through the tops of the trees.

A city explodes from the mountain. Lavish homes engraved into the mountain's rockface resemble much smaller versions of the palace itself. Layers of stone, three feet thick, square off each unit with irregular-sized bricks. Built one atop the other, they fill the mountain's side. Wooden doors carved with animals of all kinds protect their inhabitants. Jaguars for speed and agility. Condors to connect the earth to the sky, and snakes for new life.

The forest trees loom overhead and the only light shining through comes from the break in the foliage. People move about, climbing up and down the stone walkways, moving in and out of the mountain as if their home were not completely hidden from the sky.

I am ushered from the plane. We pass lush greenery and pregnant women working alongside the men. Dogs chase children in the fields and jump over irrigation canals flowing into the base of the castle. Soldiers roam the fields. They yell at the women who pause for a breath, and they yell at the children as they come near the canals. Their faces are hard. Covered in dirt and anger, they hesitate in their gait to glare at me as I move past.

My feet, too, hesitate as they approach the mouth of the castle. A man is chained to the middle of a pit. Silver shackles bleed his wrists raw. Fresh bruises line his jaw. Even from afar, the whites of his eyes hold nothing but sadness. Darius struggles against the shackles, screaming and moaning as if his fuss alone will free him. My heart sinks to the deepest pits of the earth.

My gaze lingers on him, on the sweat dripping from his bloodied bare chest. His eyes shine with anger, and he clenches his fists as he fights to pull through the metal clasp of each chain.

Although I know I should not, I turns away with responsibility eating at my gut. I did this to him, purely by stepping into his life by fate. It is my fault. My prophecy may have me chained to certain death, but chains hold Darius to the earth.

He notices me when only a few feet keep us apart. He drops his chin and shakes his head, despair seeping from each movement. He will not hold my gaze. His body sags as he drops his weight, his knees hitting the stony ground.

Cyprien watches under the grand archway, his head held high, his hands clasped behind his back. There is no smile on his face, nor in his eyes, nor in the sureness of his stance.

I kneel before Darius and wrap her hands around his shackled wrists.

"I am so sorry, Natalia." He weeps. "I am so sorry."

"For what?" I say. "I am as certain as the stars you did not ask for this. I am the one who am sorry, Darius." My grasp tightens around his palms. "You were trying to escape from all of this."

"They were waiting at the base of the driveway at the villa. I knew they wanted you, but I just couldn't allow it." His eyes reach up to meet mine. "They agreed to take me instead." He shakes his head once more. "But here you are. Not even a few hours behind me."

Cyprien approaches. He bends to me, grasping me behind the arms with a smooth and tender touch. He reaches for my hands. "I apologize for the circumstances. If I had more of a say, it would have played out very differently."

"I doubt that very much." My bluntness surprises even me, but I will not fawn or make pleasantries. My friend chained to the base of the mountain has assured that.

Cyprien tilts his head and pulls a crisp green leaf from a sheath hanging at his waist. He hands it to me. "The elevation here can be tough to get used to. For any nausea." Taking another, he hands it to Darius.

Darius pleads with me in silence, questioning the simple offering.

Recognizing the coca leaf from my childhood, I take it without question and place the crisp leaf on my tongue. Nodding my permission to Darius, he follows my lead and mimics my actions.

Cyprien lifts my hands to his lips, softly brushing a kiss across my skin. "All prophecies must hold meaning, Natalia. I fear this means we ourselves hold the weight. People need to love you. To believe in you. I, too, I must find a place for you in my heart." His gaze moves to the filling colosseum as he drops my hand. "Your sacrifice needs to hold meaning once more, my dear Natalia."

I consider the meaning of his words. I study the way his eyes hold back from me and the harshness of his voice. Compassion lingers on his face, but it is hidden behind a much harder expression I do not recognize.

"Come, let me show you to your people."

"No," I say. "My friend must go free first."

"Gaeetan has planned for it. Please, let me show you your people. "

Her eyes plead at Darius for forgiveness as I move away.

Cyprien ushers me to the pits and guides me to a small chair next to the largest of the thrones. The chairs are made of marble, shining with a glaze that reflects power and entitlement. "The farmers filing in come from the outskirts of the woods. Although they each own their own property, all profits benefit the empire."

They are a simple-looking people, dressed in sarongs and trousers much more like that of my own time.

Cyprien nods at the soldiers, each dressed in identical brown uniforms, steel ready at the draw. "The soldiers at the back hold the highest rank. They stay here in the city, keep the order, and provide us with the security and safety we need. The men in the gray are the true Iritans. They move from city to city, seeking out refuge and guidance from those who will help uphold our people's truths. Our true destinies."

The soldiers are all men, much like the soldiers of my time, much like the men who accompanied me here. Very few are younger than Cyprien himself, and very few are older than Mr. Bailey. They all stare at me. Each and every one. Hatred seeps into their eyes so deep the pits of hell could not climb out.

Taking a deep breath, I speak bluntly. "And what is the intent for Darius? Chained in the middle of your pit for all of us to watch?"

Cyprien shifts in his chair to face me. His shoulders hunch as he looks up at the stone palace. He waits with silence. The old crow, Gaeetan, lumbers to the throne chair next to him. Neither his eyes nor his movements pass over me or even acknowledge my presence.

"He is to be a demonstration," Cyprien says.

"Cyprien, please," she says. "I am here. I will do whatever you need. Please don't hurt him."

"It is not his choice, girl. " Gaeetan signals with his hand, and the soldiers move forward. A flick of the wrist and one lone soldier walks to the center of the pit. He circles Darius, enticing him.

"Please!" I scream.

The soldier lashes out and kicks Darius over and over again, then knocks him across the face.

Darius screams and swears in a language no longer familiar to me. Even with chained wrists the hatred in him is clear.

"Please, stop!" My feet push me forward, but Cyprien's hand grasps my wrist in warning. My eyes hurt to watch.

"It is for the good of our people," Cyprien says, as if assuring himself as much as me.

"Why is he being punished? I am here. I came for my people," I whisper and falls to my knees.

Cyprien's eyes dart around the mountain. The crowd sits in the pews in silence. He sweeps imaginary dirt off the shoulder of his robes, keeping himself busy amid his uncomfortable insolence.

"Darius is here to ensure that you stay. You will join the people in their day-to-day lives. Learn to love your people once more. Once they have your trust and your blood, your friend will be free to leave." Cyprien's voice is soft, but his eyes lie hard on Gaeetan.

"And if they don't learn to trust me?"

"Then he will die."

I sit quietly as I take in this knowledge. "Yes. I agree." My eyes turn to Cyprien. "Please make it stop."

"I am sorry, Natalia. But your word isn't enough." Cyprien's head jerks up to mine. "Saying something is very different than actually doing such things, of actually showing people you *can* do such things." He squints at me and lets go of my wrist. "That is why we are both here, is it not? Our words did not meet our actions?"

"Our words?" A question shines in my eyes. "What of his words? This was not his choice!"

"Choice is irrelevant."

"Is it?" I stand to tighten the laces of my boots. In and out I breath. In. Out.

"Ambition reaches beyond choice. Good or bad, we take what is ours to take."

The black leggings I wear beneath my skirt are exposed to the stares of all the men around me. With fierce movements, I tie the skirt into a knot at the base of my waist. "What you speak of is choice. Good or bad. I came here to make mine."

Stepping down from the rafters, I head straight for the center of the ring. Darius eyes me suspiciously, the chains at his wrists thick and full of dirt. The lone soldier at his side flexes his fists and stops his attack.

"Unchain him," I say.

The crowd silences.

"With all due respect, my lady, this is not negotiable." The soldier maintains a low tone, shielding the crowd from my insubordination.

"You misunderstand, my friend."

Pulling my shoulders back, I place both feet under my rib cage. I bend my knees so slightly I do not notice the transfer of weight to my thighs.

Cyprien stands and shows vigor for the first time since emerging into the dense heat of the day. For me, or for their laws, I am not quite sure. Darius closes his eyes and shakes his head in disapproval.

"I am not negotiating. Unchain him." The pressure in my fingertips rises as I clench my fists.

Darius's nose is bleeding and a black eye is already forming. Veins pop at his temples, anger covering every emotion he might be capable of. His eyes dart up to me, glistening with sadness. He shakes his head once more. "Don't do it."

The soldier is pacing behind me, but I ignore him the best I can. Darius's knees buckle and his head drops to stare at the dirt.

The angry guard at my side rushes toward me with feet heavy in the dirt. Picking that exact moment, I lunge at him. My left foot swings back just as Bailey taught me, knocking the unexpected soldier in his gut.

Jerking backwards just enough, he glances at Cyprien, hoping for guidance. Cyprien gives him none.

I use the same leg once more to sweep across his face. Blood spits into the dirt.

Closing my fist, I keep my thumb exposed and knock the man in his face. Hit after hit, his cheek bone is exposed and his blood now covers my hand. A small glimmer of blue shows at my knuckles.

Never once does he raise his arm to strike me in return. Either his permission was only for Darius, or their laws prohibit him from touching me. Regardless of the reason, I place my feet firmly on the ground. My foot connects with the core of his chest, and the man falls backward, curled like an infant on the dirt.

Cyprien glances at the broken soldier and nods to another flanked at the back of the pit. I lunge once more, striking the approaching soldier in the face. He stumbles but does not fall. He stands still and tilts his head at me, a question in his eyes. I strike his face again, and his nose swells. Dropping to his knees, tears fill his eyes. "I apologize, my lady. I did not recognize your worth."

"Do you know who I am?" I say.

"Rumors claim you were the lost sacrifice, but I thought it a lie." He turns his reddened cheeks to the crowd. "But I know now for certain. Only a woman of your stature could be meant for an afterlife with the gods."

Placing my palms on my knees for support, I take deep breaths to steady my fear and not crumble to the ground. I force my eyes to stay open.

"My life is meant to save yours from this volcano. My life is offered to the God of Light. For you." My voice shakes with anger. I point at Darius. "This man is not to be touched."

The soldier searches Cyprien's face for reassurance.

A simple nod from Cyprien, and the soldier unbinds Darius's wrists. He stumbles slightly, pressing his palm against the dirt as he stands.

My desire to end his beating rages inside my chest. I pain for him, for his loss, and for his own sacrifices. A sacrifice he did not choose.

"Anything else?" Cyprien says.

"I was promised as a queen. I could at least be treated like one until my time has come to pass."

Cyprien's eyes watch me. His lips turn up in admiration. He nods his head once more as Gaeetan huffs and grumbles at his side.

Standing straight, I untie the knot in my skirt and wipe the blood off her hand. Firmly pressing on my knuckles, I hide the blue shimmer from anyone's view.

I kneel in front of Darius and plead with him. "Stand and follow me. Whatever you do. Do not look back."

Standing from my crouch, I turn to the throne. I pull my shoulders back and face Cyprien and Gaeetan. "Now, if you don't mind, I had a long journey. I am ready to be shown my chambers." Dropping my skirt, I steal a moment to look at the wide eyes of the crowd, and back to the shattered man at my feet.

Cyprien nods, a slight grin on his face. I turn and stomp into the stone castle that now becomes my fortress.

Chapter Thirty-One
Quinn

They left the Jeep after the second day, the trail no longer drivable, and began their tedious trek into the forest. They continue in silence. Quinn is grateful no one wishes to discuss the weather or the prospects of a successful outcome.

The underbrush grows thicker as the day moves on, and the thorns that stick into his pant legs become more annoying than ever. Ryan, with more muscle than Bailey and more expertise than Quinn, takes the lead and lashes a path as best he can.

There is something about the forest Quinn secretly admires more than digging in the dirt or finding fresh relics. The forest has a peace to it. It has always been a place that helps Quinn connect to his thoughts, discover his inner desires, or reflect on past pains. Today, Quinn thinks of Natalia growing up in such a place, beauty and calmness surrounding each direction of the earth. The silence of it isn't even true silence at all. It is a whisper in the wind, the hum of bugs too excited to see another venture into the territory. It is a reconnection with what is real and everything that could be real.

Although the trek is a laborious journey, it is still manageable. Finding a place to camp becomes much more difficult. The brush is at its fullest in August, and open terrain is limited. Clearing out as much brush as possible, they worry more about crawling creatures and animals with fangs than shelter from the night.

They make their way to a dip in the ground and follow a river.

"Do we have a plan once we get there?" Ryan says as they continue searching for smooth ground.

"Yea, we get Natalia and leave," Quinn says.

"No," Bailey says. "She chose to go. She needs our support. Fear makes her choices right now. We need to be there for clarity."

"You're crazy old man," Quinn says. "I am not going there to support her. Not when it means sacrifice and false pretenses of happily ever after."

"There won't be a happily ever after, and we all know that. Even she knows that."

"Then what are we supporting?"

"Her. We support her until she sees what nonsense this is and that they are crazy ass sons of bitches. She's gonna see the cursed souls of those people herself. I'm sure of it, and we'll be there for her to lean on when she realizes exactly what her father realized."

"That she is better than them," Ryan says.

"And what if they don't let her leave so willingly?" Quinn says.

"When the time comes, that is when we will figure out a plan."

"You know, if I went to school more often I might be able to think more critically about this."

Ryan tosses a stump out of their way and snorts. "If you went to school more, you wouldn't have fallen head over heels for a girl eight-hundred times your age."

Bailey chuckles. "Or start drooling like a lost puppy dog each time she enters a room."

Quinn stops walking as both men begin to laugh. He scowls at them. "I do not drool. Seriously, I do not."

"You do, kid." Ryan turns around and puts a hand on Quinn's shoulder. "So let's make you more loveable than the scary, dark Iritan guy. Okay?"

"This is not matchmaking."

He brushes Ryan's hand off his shoulder and stalks away.

Bailey continues to laugh despite their need for quiet in the forest. But their argument was so loud they neglected to pay attention to the surrounding wildlife. Quinn, a quarter-mile in front, finally notices the eerie silence. A simple buzz or flutter would soothe his thoughts more at that moment.

Stopping abruptly, he turns, his face white as a stone. Ryan and Bailed stop murmuring and laughing when they notice Quinn's panic, his tormented stillness.

A nest of anacondas, their dark green color camouflaging into the foliage, hang over his head. Two rows of black spots intertwine with white marking on their sides. Coils wrap around the branches at least six meters long.

He counts two sets of eyes, each with a tongue lashing out, searching for his scent. Tangled into one another, he can't tell where one snake begins and the other ends. "I really didn't want to die today," he whispers.

The snakes ignore Ryan and Bailey and transfix on Quinn. His presence irritates them.

The two men back up slowly. Bailey's eyes catch Quinn's and urge him not to make another sound as the two snakes begin to unwrap themselves from the branches and slither toward him.

With the humidity thick on his face, he considers running. Basking in the sun may slow them down, but he fears the forest mud would hinder his escape.

Shaking, he reaches into his back pocket and grasps the scale

Natalia left him. He thinks of her and the puma. Just like the snakes, she knew it was there before anyone else. She felt the fear and was left with little escape. The feline only had eyes on her. The cat clawed through to her blue blood but ignored the other men.

With shaky hands, he unbuttons his back pocket and pulls out the dragon scale. The snakes freeze, as if in a trance that can't be broken.

Unsure what to do next, and not wanting to lose the scale, he moves his arm to the side, his grasp tight. The snakes' heads follow the motion, like a drug to a heroin addict. Bailey's heart beats so fast Quinn swears he can see his chest rise and fall from ten meters away.

Unwilling to lose the whole thing, Quinn peels the scale into two. Second guessing himself, he peels one of the halves in two as well. He places the smallest piece on the ground and hides the other two pieces in his pocket.

With the snakes still frozen, Quinn steps back, one foot at a time. Knowing a simple trip of his feet or dip in the dirt could lead to his demise, he turns his back on the snakes. He would rather it happen at his rear than watch death come straight on. The idea of such a cowardly approach humbles him, knowing it is the opposite of everything Natalia has faced. His steps become more forceful as his anger at himself rises. She stares death in the face, and he tiptoes away from it.

He turns to face the snakes and gasps. The snakes have sheltered the scale, their bodies a mountain on top of the small piece of flesh. Their heads rest upon each other. They appear to slumber, no longer concerned for Quinn or his actions.

Ryan and Bailey circle around to his side and lead him deeper into the forest.

Chapter Thirty-Two
Natalia

I am shown to a room at the west end of the castle while Darius is escorted to the east. Although promised his safety, I clench my teeth as is he escorted away. I should have insisted he remain closer. I should have done so many things differently. If only I could truly protect the people I care for.

Within my room, I find the solitude I would have found as a child. Privacy. Silence. Even a wardrobe full of clothes. The down-covered bed is large enough for an entire family.

I sit on the side of the bed and study the woven patterns on the green and black tapestries on the walls. The colors of the earth spread across the room like a shield. Green for the earth. Black for our ancestors. How could a textile hold so much more meaning than my past?

Alone in my room, my thoughts hold on Darius. He was pulled so much deeper into this mess while only trying to move further and further away from it. And why? To be beaten and chained? To be held here like a hostage, kept from living his free will? He deserves so much better.

My silence and solitude do not last. A heavy knock pounds on the door. The solid wood thunders a demand and the guard flings the door open before even waiting for my response. "Come," is all he states. I pull myself up and hide my annoyance at his bedside manners. As he begins to walk down the hall, I am expected to follow behind. I am escorted to dinner with Cyprien. My escort, a man of great height, does not look at me as he leads me down the hall. I struggle to keep up with his brisk pace.

The halls resemble what I expect to see in the interior of a mountain. The stone floors are paved smooth. Marble columns with intricate designs and markings are positioned along the passageways. My eyes have never witnessed such beauty. With that beauty, however, comes the darkness of a windowless castle. Candelabras maintain luminated paths, and crystal chandeliers cast sparkles over the floors.

The quaint room I am taken to is darker than my bedchambers. A long rectangular table fills the room, the strong smell of the wood overpowering the aroma of food in the kitchens.

Cyprien sits at the head of the table, a fire roaring in the brick fireplace at his rear. I am seated at the other end of the table. My escort's hate for me remains clear as he pardons himself from my side and rushes away. I doubt I would have received a pardon if Cyprien had not been in my company.

Cyprien stares at me for several minutes before rising from his seat. He walks to my side and pulls out a chair beside me. He places two crystal glasses and a bottle of wine on the table in front of us.

The wine smells heavily of oak, bringing a memory of my father. I think of him now, wondering what his thoughts would have been of me at this table. Or of the man next to me, with sternness in his name, yet apprehension in his posture.

"You surprised me today," he says as he sits. "In many ways actually." Looking at me expectantly, I remain quiet.

Anger still fills my veins while eagerness composes my thoughts.

"When I heard you were coming, I originally thought it a mistake. The last time we met you made it very clear you were not interested."

My silence coats the walls.

"And to my wonder, you arrive with a spring in your step. Soldiers have been disobedient for months. You show up, and they kneel at your feet."

I shift in my chair, crossing my legs at the ankles, and fold the crease in her skirt under my hips. "One man is very different than that of a disobedient population."

He pours wine into his glass. "Maybe so. Either way, I'm thankful." He holds up his glass. "To a fresh start. I hope you are able to provide that for us." He offers me the empty glass.

I shake my head with a slight tilt of my neck. "No, thank you."

He pours me a glass anyway.

The red liquid runs ripples down the inside of the glass, reminding me of every impurification I was ever taught to avoid, every act of rebellion punishable by death.

"I need your help, Natalia," he whispers.

It is the tone more than the words that make me look at him. I have always thought of him as the descendent of darkness, a prince caught in the world of hateful grudges. But now, I am not so sure. The possibility of humanity hides itself behind his vivid jawline, masking the dark circles under his eyes. He does not seem the same man I met at the dragon carving in the village. He is not the same threatening man stalking me to Estancia, or even the disinterested, privileged prince watching an innocent man during a beating. At this moment, sitting next to me in a spot of honor at the table, and asking me to relinquish and savor a beverage foreign to my tongue, he seems exposed. Maybe even fearful. Certainly vulnerable.

"Our beliefs are lost. We have forgotten our virtues. Our strengths as a people." He takes a long drink.

I consider his words. In his silence, I find the strength to pick up my own glass.

In a time not so far from my distant memories, I am not sure I would have ever been allowed to relish the taste of wine. Coca leaves at my death, perhaps. But I was always meant to stay pure, pure for the gods, pure for my king. And for what? For my pure heart to twist with hatred at my stolen youth? To have my life stolen away from every commitment I have ever faced? I fear it was all for nothing. I fear my wasted life will end in ruin at the tip of this very mountain. Without understanding why, or considering the unforetold outcomes, I stare at the red liquid sitting in front of me.

I take a sip. The wine burns as it slips down my throat, and I immediately desire more to savor in my mouth.

"Are you going to ask me how?"

"How, Cyprien? How am I to help you?" The sarcasm feels thick on my tongue. Thick and pleasant, much like the wine left in my glass.

He ignores my contempt and continues with pleasantries. Forced for pure, I am not quite sure. "Just by being here, I hope."

Two dishes of lamb are brought to the table as he speaks. The steam rises from the meat like the shine of the full moon. They smell of fresh herbs and savory lentils.

"Even today, you did what I couldn't. Not even Gaeetan could. You gave those people optimism."

Cutting the lamb piece by piece, he seems to savor the juices in his mouth. His eyes close with each bite, and it makes me wonder how often he receives meals such as this.

"Today was not really about Darius, you see. It was about everyone watching. A test, if you will."

"Why? Why would that be necessary?"

Cyprien pours me a second glass of wine before I even begin her meal.

Deflecting my question, he finishes his glass of wine. "Why did you come?"

Picking up my fork, my eyes harden. My heart becomes a rock of stone and I forget every reason I thought this man pleasant. "You killed my friend. I was scared for the rest of them."

His eyes scrunch, the frown on his mouth touching my thoughts. "I am sorry, Natalia, but I did no such thing. Although, I truthfully wouldn't put it past Gaeetan."

Without responding, I place a piece of lamb in my mouth.

"Who was it? The boy?"

That is when my head snaps up. Warmth from my chest forces heat to my skin. My eyes are confused. "No, Santino."

He is silent for a brief moment, considering my words. "I am so sorry for your loss. I hope you will understand that I did not kill your friend."

With his lips thinned and his eyes closed, a sentiment in him I fear I missed before becomes viable. My father once told me that a person's eyes tell the story of their soul. To truly understand their heart, you need to look for the reflection in their eyes. Cyprien closes his eyes so often I can't help but wonder who he is shutting out.

I nod at him, only partly believing he had nothing to do with Santino's murder, and we finish their meal in silence. My heart reaches for an understanding that does not come. I drink for each of my unanswered questions. I enjoy the weight it lifts from my head and heart, and the warmth that trails down my throat.

The more I drink, the easier I find Cyprien's company. He does not radiate evil. As a man on his own, he seems to understand my need for quiet company.

As our plates are cleared, he finally smiles at me. A soft smile that expresses understanding. Concern. "Please, let me escort you to bedchamber. It must be getting late."

Stumbling to my feet, I accept his arm. My feet feel heavy, and I am forced to lean on him more than I would under normal circumstances. Perhaps I have misjudged him and misread the entire situation.

I wish it were Quinn I were learning on, his muscular arms under my own with the smell of pine emanating off him. I wish it were Quinn I dined with, his smile lingering on me each time he filled my glass.

That is what I think of as my bedroom door is opened for me, as the heat of my flesh brushes on the skin next to me, his face inches away from my own, his breath warming my cheek. Does he, too, think I am someone else? Am I more than just a girl trapped in his castle?

I let his hands linger up my back, the pressure of his palms wrinkling my dress. My pulse quickens as I feel the heat of his exhale against the nape of my neck. His hands move down the length of my back, wrap around my abdomen, and hold me firm at the hips. Touch is venomous and I instantly understand why I was kept separate from the world.

I imagine the blue of his hair mingling with the blue in my veins releasing the magic that has been dead for centuries. I think of his olive skin as I help pull off his shirt. His strong muscles keep my feet on the ground, my boots on the ground. The boots with frayed laces. The laces Quinn taught me how to tie.

I pull away from Cyprien so fast I startle not only him, but myself as well. The shock in his eyes reflects out of my own. My eyes search his for empathy, for compassion. But he is unreadable, as always.

Reaching down to pick his thrown shirt off the ground, he pauses, and ties the lace on my boot as if he knows that is where my thoughts rest: on a pair of boots that are too badass to be sacrificed to a fire or thrown into a mountain. They belong on the floor next to another set like their own, not beside golden slippers too precious to step down from a throne without a chaperone.

"I'm sorry," I whisper. "I have never been allowed to drink wine before. It must have gotten the best of me."

"It is me who must apologize, Natalia. You need more time."

Cyprien's influence over me is menacing. Unnatural. Pulling the shirt over his head, he closes the door behind him, leaving me secluded once more with shameful thoughts. Sorrow fills my eyes, and I cry myself to sleep.

Chapter Thirty-Three
Quinn

When the river becomes a swamp at their feet, they know they need to move to higher, dry ground, but with the mountain so close, they are afraid their path must follow the wetlands. They compromise and circle around the water the best they can, now more than ever keeping a close eye out for wildlife.

When their socks are drenched and their bellies rumble, they finally see evidence of hope. Smoke tunnels rise into the sky. The smell of wet leaves burning into ash overcomes their senses.

Passing through a small clearing, the village they approach is quaint. Homes are made of clay, with the jungle resting layers upon layers to hide rooftops from the sky above.

The villagers are gathered in groups, several around the fire, more under the coverings of tented rooftops. The men carve wood into animals with tusks and fangs larger than their palms. The women weave baskets and laugh at the children running in circles at their feet. Dressed simply in loose white linen, the children wear next to nothing, unaware of modesty in their seclusion from the modern world.

The daily activities of the tribe stop at their approach, and they are eyed nervously. Everyone watches them. A few men pull out spears pointed in their direction. Their tense frames hold on to something much worse than fear for their people.

With Bailey in the lead, Ryan and Quinn hold strong. They walk into the center of the village, past the men holding spears, past the children finding refuge behind their mothers' quaking legs.

"We are looking for a girl. We are worried for her safety and wish to take her home." Bailey's words ring out loud and clear. Nearly thirty tribesmen gather to hear.

A small man with bare feet and gray hair walks past the burning fires and faces Bailey. "There is no girl that passed."

"Please," Bailey says. "She is Natalia of Estancia. Her blood runs blue."

Every head in the tribe turns to that of the old man. The men, the women, even the small children stop building stones in the dirt. Their linen is flushed with dirt, but their eyes hold a brightness not even Quinn can grasp.

The people are quiet, a stillness the wind refuses to rustle against. More people gather and time stops, creating an awkward silence that troubles Quinn.

The old man moves inches from their faces. The smell of eucalyptus teases the pores on Quinn's face.

"Does she fly? This blue treasure you're looking for?" the old man says.

"Yes. Yes, she does."

"You must come with me." Without question they follow, his leadership never denied.

The entire tribe follows the old man as he leads the newcomers past their homes and up dirt paths at the rear of the village. But as the old man enters the cave hidden behind the village, the rest of the villagers stop. Only Bailey, Ryan, and Quinn follow him inside.

A torch is lit to squeeze out the darkness.

Why doesn't he feel fear? Or at least confusion? Is she here? Trapped in this cave? Did they find her too late? Or is it something this tribe fears so much more?

They follow a dark path of stalactites and water drippings. Rocks are translucent under the light of the torch's flame, and the stones are slick at their feet. They follow the old man as he tangles them up in a maze of tunnels in a cave the size of a city block.

The tunnels narrow and become steeper the farther they go, and the air grows wet and cold. The tunnels squeeze narrower and often require the mean to side step their way through.

Quinn breathes harder and harder, and his pulse finds it difficult to keep pace.

They finally stop in front of a wall larger than the mountain itself. A room has opened up into a small alcove, large enough to fit one hundred men. The wall is carved with beautiful and intricate designs, like a timeline, and the story unfolds across the wall, each frame carved deep into the rock.

"I ask you, as men from beyond the jungle," the old man croaks. "Does your blue treasure hold the same story as ours?"

The pictures tell of two groups of people fighting. A young girl is presented, and the fighting subsides. As the child grows, one group watches over her while the other turns to darkness. The moon becomes black, and the people begin to suffer. They grow in numbers, but their eyes fill with darkness.

The girl vanishes in the night, and the first group of people are massacred in response. Only a few escape the bloodshed and build their own sheltered village hidden in the jungle. They remain few, but they prosper. And they survive.

The darkness reigns over the mountain until one day the lost girl emerges from the thick of the jungle. Her fires burn away the darkness, and the flames rebuild the sunshine that had been lost for so long. She leads her people out of the jungle and rebuilds their empire. Watching. Protecting. Defeating the darkness once and for all.

"Are you Kinoda?" Quinn says.

The old man drops to his knees and stretches his hands before him. "We have been many things. Many, many things. But we have not been Kinodan for nearly a thousand years." He wipes his worn face with his shaky hands. His eyes glimmer in the torchlight. "Please. Please tell me, has she emerged from the jungle?"

Quinn's joints nearly buckle beneath him. The man speaks of Natalia.

"Only if we do something to get her back," Bailey says. "We fear she has walked straight into the mountain."

Chapter Thirty-Four
Natalia

I spend the next several days hidden under the comfortable confines of my bedcovers. Too embarrassed to leave, too ashamed to move. I cower from my choices and cower from the smoking mountain. Cyprien forces me to dinner each night but allows me to eat in silence without passing judgment. He says not a word.

Each day passes the same as the last, dining with Cyprien and crying myself to sleep. But I no longer accept the wine.

Cyprien is not wicked and he could be kind. He is someone I could marry if only my marriage to him held a future. But a future is pointless. I know better to dream of such things. And even then…if I were to allow myself to dream, there are far better ones I would allow than Cyprien.

On the sixth day, I exit the confines of my room and wander the paths in the village in search of Darius. The villagers stand rigid at first, refusing to look at me. They turn their backs when I peruse the trinkets in their market. The drop their heads as I walk past.

I see the temptation in their gait, their desire to stop hating me. They are polite when I speak or ask questions of the food in their baskets. Do they hate me of their own free will or because of expectations from the king? Do they even know why they are to hate me? Have they seen my friend? Do they know if he is well? Safe?

The farmers treat me quite differently than the villagers. Their knees drop to the ground in front of me. They place offerings in my arms, refusing to take payment for their gifts of cotton and obsidian. They do not look me in the eye out of hatred but out of respect and a long-held tradition to honor my name. To them, I am a queen. They tell me Darius is well but kept in the confines of his room. He is fed but kept under lock and key. He has not been allowed out.

I question my every move. What must I do to help my friend? How to I regain the trust of a village, of all its members, even the ones who show me such distaste? Hiding in my room is surely no longer an option. I must submit to my promises and become one with the people. My people. To earn their trust, I must be seen. And they need to trust me, or Darius will not go free.

So, I do what I know I must, and become one of the people. I spend most of my days in the market helping to sort produce. I help the men unload crops from barrels and hand out water to the men and woman returning from the fields. I work with them, eat with them, and sweat with them. I walk in their fields, down their streets, and rest in their shade.

The villagers begin to soften over time. Although they do not speak directly to me, they stop turning their backs, and many pause or linger near my path when I sing her way through the square.

I pick songs of peace and earn my keep in order to give meaning to my future sacrifice, just as Cyprien had once asked of me. And it works. Slowly, I am accepted. I become one of their own. Only once did my songs find passage to the dragons, and Gaeetan appeared at my side instantaneously. I was dragged her into the confines of the castle like a child being reprimanded for misbehaviors.

The message was received and understood. I am not to sing of dragons.

Gaeetan's actions that day softened the people's opinion of me and put me on even footing with the rest of them. I become more than the girl to hate like they hated Gaeetan. Fear follows the eyes of each and every villager when he appears. His station is clear. It is his village. It is his rule.

The women stop staring me down, the farmers smile at me with their eyes, and the children bow and curtsey at me. But the guards do not. I wish they would soften to me as well.

How much did the children know of me, and why their king plots my death? I consider how the world has changed, how the people have changed. For with all that change, could my sacrifice truly make a difference? Could these people prosper and find more love and kindness in their hearts with my death? Could Gaeetan?

From time to time, farmers are chained to the center pits. They are beaten and tortured for things out of their control: food supplies dwindle, the rain is too hard, the weather too hot. Kindness has disappeared from the old king's mind.

Each time, the men fight against the guards with hatred in their souls. They scream and they resist while the villagers are forced to watch. They spit obscenities at the king, only to find more beatings in response.

I find it hard not to hate along with them when the laws are backwards, and the choices of their leaders do not make sense. He is a king of hatred. Lacking compassion or soul, he rules because he can and that is the only message he sends to his people.

Day after day, I rise to my feet when I see too much and ask them to stop. I insist the guards return to their stations and leave the farmers to suffer in peace. Although I have found a place for these people in my heart, it is difficult to make the request. Even the guard who kneeled at my feet the day of my arrival does what he must because of his king's orders. If only the guards had the strength to think for themselves. The torment is no longer about the farmers, nor the rain or the food, it is about me.

As each man falls, Cyprien stands taller, and his eyes tell me that my assumptions are correct. It is not the men and their bad luck that brought them to the pits in the dirt. Darius was just the first of a line of unknowing men lined up in Gaeetan's thoughts. They were brought there for me. Because of me. To prove myself to the empire over and over again. To prove I will do what it takes. I will save them. All of them. Even if I am the cause of their pain.

I confront Gaeetan on a day cooler than most. "Why are the guards not punished for their part?"

"That's preposterous," Gaeetan mumbles. "It is not their fault the will of the farmers is weak."

"I beg to differ. If they were good at their jobs, their will would prosper just as your land."

He considers me a moment, his eyes wandering over the gathering of people at his side. The stance of the guards holds stronger than that of the farmers. Colder. Their hatred of me is still clear. I see it in their eyes, the way they hold themselves next to me, as if I am poison. A viper from the pits of the jungle.

"They could kill you," Cyprien whispers, so only she can hear.

"Aren't they going to eventually anyway? Besides, if you want me to make a difference, it's your guards that need to break," I whisper back.

Gaeetan hears and snarls. "You are not in charge here! Your

blood is the only thing that can save these people. It has been owed to them since the day they were born." He points his walking stick up the mountain. "The longer you live, the longer these people will suffer!"

For that, I have no reply.

Gaeetan pelts me across the face. The sting, a sensation new and unexpected. "The people suffer because of you! You denied them the future they were promised!"

Cyprien approaches Gaeetan turning his head to me in warning. His eyes plead for me not to speak. He places one hand on the old man's shoulder and calms the muscles in his neck. "That is enough." His voice is flat. "Her blood is no different from yours, old man."

"My blood is the only blood that remains pure!" Pointing his walking cane at Cyprien, his voice becomes cold. "Even you have blood mixed with the enemy!"

"Come, I think it is time for you to rest."

"I am tired of resting! Let her blood spill and be done with it! What are you even waiting for? Just do it!"

His anger and barbarity pulls at my heartstrings, and I finally understand why the people hold so much anger and resentment in their hearts.

"What are all of you waiting for?" he bellows across the arena.

"She will not die just to make a point. I will not allow it." Cyprien's voice remains calm despite Gaeetan's trembles, though his bravado weakens as he approaches the shaking old man.

"I have been waiting my whole life for this, you stupid boy! The spill of her blood belongs to me!"

I see it in his eyes, eyes replaced by the memory of a king. A king I wore shoes for when my very own toes screamed against it.

I see the mask of hatred replaced by something else in the dilation of his pupils, a revenge so primitive it clutches at my chest and echoes in my blood. It was the same fear I held the moment in the square when we first met. He hates me far more than anyone would ever understand.

"Come, let me take you to your chambers," Cyprien says.

"Do not force me to kill you for merely getting in my way first," Gaeetan mumbles to Cyprien. "You have until the full moon. I will not stand for a moment longer."

"Very well. Horace, please escort my grandfather to his chambers. It seems as though the heat is getting to him."

The hush of the crowd continues as Gaeetan is taken inside, huffing and puffing along the way. His feet barely hold his small frame up without the help of Horace, the silent guard who hates me just as much as he seems to hate Gaeetan. He pulls Gaeetan along, squeezing his arm.

But it is not the public argument that I consider as the crowd finally disperses. It is not the anger that Gaeetan holds so tightly, or the guards who hate him nearly as much as I do. No, it was the drip of blue blood that Gaeetan wiped from his nose as he walked away.

Dragon blue mixed in the red oils of deceit.

Chapter Thirty-Five
Quinn

Kinodans seem a simple people at first sight. Their homes are unpretentious. Some huts have straw roofs, while others have wooden troughs and banisters symbolizing a much deeper understanding of woodworking than what originally meets the eye.

Their village lies in a circle with the huts bordering the edge of the jungle. Rubber trees stretch into the sky like ladders, and buckets hang on the thick branches to collect the trees' sap.

Each and every tree encircling the village is tapped and the milky liquid flows. Latex must remain the focus of trade, although who profits when their village is hidden in the forest is a big question.

Higher-ranking people live in wooden cabins close to the center, while those on the village's edge live in sod huts. But in a group without differences in economic standing, what creates the tier system? Quinn just can't seem to figure it out.

The central camp fire rests in the middle of the village with half a dozen trails spiraling off to the caves, but the people never move to that side of the camp. They always stay away from the caves.

Quinn wanders the camp as the village supper is being prepared. The children run barefoot, laughing and playing, and the women and men are busy in their day-to-day duties. They seem like a happy people. God knows he wouldn't be smiling and laughing as he pressed clothes clean or carried water on top of his head.

He makes his way to the dining hall with its massive wooden doors, and the chimneys that spew smoke and the smell of fish into the air.

The people wait outside the doors. Quinn joins them and waits patiently for Bailey and Ryan to return from refreshing themselves after their day. Jealous of their prolonged appearance, he picks at the dirt under his nails. He should have taken more time to relish in the soap and water provided for him.

As soon as the doors open, people saunter into the gathering hall like distracted snails. While he can barely push his way fast enough to the tables, the women next to him stop to laugh and embrace. His patience recedes at the sound of his stomach grumbling.

Rice in banana leaves cover the tables. Fish are piled high in wooden bowls held together with cinnamon sticks.

His mouth waters for the passion fruit, and he sits just as his companions arrive, clean-shaven and odorless.

Song and dance erupt as dinner begins. Half of the people ignore the meal and prance around the hall.

The three men sit aside, fairly isolated, and eat their meals while they watch the festivities.

"Seems as though we are celebrating does it not?" Bailey says.

"What is it they are celebrating, exactly?" Quinn says. "Our unexpected arrival or their savior in the clutches of the enemy?"

"Perhaps the reappearance of their savior?" Ryan says.

While they eat, their eyes wander to the villagers. They smile and laugh as they eat. The men sit apart from the woman, holding soft conversations of their own. The children sit upon their mother's laps and eat from the same place. There are no dishes set at the table. Their fruit holds their meals, soaking in the flavors of the forest.

As they finish their meals, the old tribal leader, Waura, makes way to their table, and pats Bailey on the back. "Please, all of you, join me outside for a smoke."

Outside, Waura sits himself in front of the central fire, and urges Bailey, Quinn, and Ryan to do the same. He sits on a smoothed rock. His bare feet warming by the flames of the fire.

He smiles as he lights his pipe, and smoke rises high above his head. "What a joyous day is it not?"

Although the three of them nod and grin, Quinn wonders once more why the day is so joyous. Natalia is still missing, either in the heart of the jungle by herself or waiting to be seduced by the enemy.

"War leaders have all agreed. Training begins in the morning." Taking another puff from his pipe, he lifts his chin up to the sky. "We will go to her. We will rescue Natalia of Estancia and bring her home."

"Home?" Quinn says. "Where exactly do you presume that is?"

"Why, here of course." He spreads his arms. "She will bring us good fortune and light up our darkened nights."

"It seems as though your people prosper greatly. How is it your nights are darkened?" Bailey says.

Waura sighs. "Since the turn of time, our people have been cursed. We do not fare well when we leave the jungle. Natalia is our key. She has always been our key."

Quinn thinks of their tapped trees, their sod houses, and their delicious fish. Village chores are completed quickly and joyously. But also, kindness. He does not believe a curse keeps them here, but pride that forces them out. "Do you have many warriors?"

"Not many, no," Waura mumbles. "But that changes tomorrow. Tomorrow we will all become warriors."

Quinn leans in to Ryan. "I thought we were just going to support her?"

"Are you suggesting that war is not supportive?" Ryan says.

"Are you saying that it is? 'Cause I say, no. Not at all. Seems to me it's time for us to talk to Pops. We need a new plan."

Chapter Thirty-Six
Natalia

"I need to see Darius." I approach Cyprien early in the day, before he has time to become flustered with his grandfather's bad attitude or annoyed with the guard's poor choices towards the farmers.

"No. Gaeetan would not allow it." His eyes sweep to mine, but do not linger.

"I must go, Cyprien. It is neither a question nor a request," I say.

"No. He would have my head."

"Then don't tell him. You said yourself you are the one to succeed him. So, start making decisions in the here and now. It's not like he is going to live forever, Cyprien." I test the waters with my statement, looking for a response.

Cyprien turns his body and gives me his full attention. "But he lives now. And no one, not even me, goes against his wishes."

I take a step closer to him. I am not scared of this man. Not in his resentful eyes or the blood of his worthless grandfather. He does as he is told much as I did my whole life. He was taught to follow orders and to be Gaeetan's pawn. So that is exactly what he does.

"I will go with or without you, Cyprien. The only difference is whether I get caught or not. Without you, I get caught, and I put all blame on you."

"And if I take you and he will still find out. He finds out everything."

"Then you can blame me. Tell him I bribed you or blackmailed you. Or whatever. I honestly don't really care what you tell him."

He tilts his head in thought and looks around at all the guards positioned randomly throughout the arena.

"You are a pain in my ass. Since the moment you fell into our lives, you have been a giant pain in my ass." He grabs my wrist and begins pulling me towards the castle. His grip is firm, but his eyes are soft. Annoyed, but kind.

"She is on my last nerve today, Horace. Make sure no one comes looking for her today, would ya?" Horace winks as Cyprien and I walk past, through the arched doors and into the musty cold of the mountain. He walks me past a series of hallways and passageways unfamiliar to my typical walks. He takes me through darkened rooms and over stone floors that have been forgotten to be washed.

We stop at a lone door, at the end of the darkened hall. "Ten minutes. You have ten minutes tops." He lets go of my wrist, warning thick in his voice.

I don't knock on the door, but I open it slowly, a little scared of what I might find. Is he being treated well? Has he been fed? Has he already lost all hope?

"Darius? Darius, are you here?" I walk into the room to see him sitting on the floor, a blanket wrapped around his shoulders. His face holds the remnants of black and blue bruises, but the color of his eyes holds an energy only food and nourishments could produce.

He drops the blanket to the ground, and rushes to the door. He picks me up in his arms just as the door closes shut behind me. My arms squeeze around him.

"Are you alright?" I say

"I am fine."

"Are they treating you fairly?"

"The guards are pretty big assholes. But the moment that kid stepped in and threatened to throw them off the mountain they have left me alone."

"Cyprien?"

"I know. I was surprised too." He takes a step back to get a clear look at my face. "Tell me your plan, Natalia. How are we getting out of here?"

"I do what they say."

"Natalia, that is a really shitty plan." Darius says.

I smile at him despite myself. "It's a plan that gets you home. That is all that matters."

"No. It's not all that matters. We need a plan that has us leaving here together."

"My life is an anomaly, Darius. But yours has just begun. I will do everything I can and you must trust that what happens is my trying to make right. Gaeetan is the key. I am sure of it."

"I don't trust him, Natalia. There is something very off about him."

"More than any of us could probably imagine. But I need you to do me a favor, Darius."

"Anything, just name it and I will get it done." He says.

"Go back to Mr. Bailey. Go back to Quinn and go back to Ryan. Tell them I am sorry I never said goodbye." His body goes rigid , his mouth quiet. Cyprien opens the door a crack and motions with his fingers my need to hurry. My time is up. I embrace my friend once more and walk away from Darius without listening for his reply. Without telling him of my true plan or my true concerns. But I also leave him with purpose. And purpose is often then only thing that helps us keep moving forward.

Chapter Thirty-Seven
Quinn

Wauna wasn't kidding when he said training starts in the morning. They are pulled awake before the sun even begins to peek through the trees. They are fitted for swords and handed shields made of iron. All around the camp young boys and young men practice their swings. They look at their footing, and the adjust each other's movements.

The women work at the side. They bang their rocks on the iron of the swords and sharpen their blades the best they know how. The children paint the shields. They paint insignias of green and red and hold their brushes with pride. Everyone participates. Everyone takes part and everyone prepares for the fight ahead.

Bailey grabs the sword placed in Quinn's hand and raises his voice at Wauna. "He is not to have a sword!"

"A man without a sword is surely a man who dies." Wauna states.

"Quinn will not fight in this war."

"What is a man who does not fight in a war?" Wauana says.

"None of your men have ever been in a war! Isn't that why you train? Isn't that why you got up before dawn to teach them some sort of resemblance to a military attack?"

"War has come. Our men fight or they leave as cowards."

"There doesn't need to be a war. We can figure this out. We can get her out a different way," Bailey says.

Wauna's eyes become hard. "If you choose to stay, you must fight. Otherwise you must leave." Wauna turns and walks out of sight. He determination sticks in the air.

"Pops, you know I can fight. You have made sure of it since I was a kid. You don't need to worry about me," Quinn says.

"Of course, I worry about you! This isn't about a boxing match, Quinn! This is about people out for blood. I am not sending you out there with a sword in your damn hand!"

"But I am going. And you know that. No matter what you do or what you say, I am going. Don't you think I go as prepared as possible? Hope for the best but still know how to survive if I need to?"

"This isn't about survival, Quinn! You're going to end up doing something stupid and I won't have it!"

"I know. Pops, I know." Quinn drops the shield in his hand and takes a step closer to him. "But they are our only chance. We can't leave her there. We can't." Bailey is silent as Ryan approaches, cautiously aware of a disagreement between father and son.

"I don't want you on the ground playing with swords." His tone is flat. Final.

"Then let's compromise." Ryan puts his hands in his pockets and looks between the two stubborn faces. "Teach him to use a bow and arrow. And make him stay high in the trees."

Quinn and Bailey keep their eyes on the forest floor but nod their heads in agreement nevertheless.

So Quinn learns how to use a bow and arrow while Bailey learns to fight with a sword. Ryan, does both, always the overachiever. Quinn's aim gets better with each arrow he lets fly. He imagines his target as one minute closer to Natalia. Because the waiting is infuriating him. How do they even know they have time to train? What if they are already too late?

Chapter Thirty -Eight
Natalia

I begin to track Gaeetan's movements, noticing for the first time how he never shows up for meals. He is absent from the pits for days on end and he is never in his rooms without guards posted at his doors.

I try mapping out the castle in my mind, determined to identify how to get in and out without being noticed. Cyprien claims I am not a prisoner, but guards are constantly at my beck and call. They become annoyed whenever I request a walk outside the walls or a tour inside the castle. I know my time is limited with the full moon's approach and fear I may have been outwitted.

"Why does Gaeetan never dine with us?" I say to Cyprien over a course of roasted boar.

He puts his fork down. "I fear he does not like you, my dear."

"Why does he not make daily visits to the pits? It seems as though it's an expectation for everyone else?"

"As I am sure you have noticed, his health is not steady. My grandfather is very, very, old."

"How old is he?"

Cyprien picks up his fork once more, looking away from me as if I had never spoken.

"How old is he?" I say again.

Cyprien pauses mid-bite and squints at me.

I stand up and push my chair in place against the table. "You see … I myself have questioned my true age." Gliding my finger around the table's edge, I walk the length of the room, my dinner forgotten. "Your age, however, holds no confusion, is that correct?"

Putting down his fork, Cyprien reclines in his chair. Crossing his arms across his chest, his voice becomes hard. "No, Natalia. There is no confusion over my age."

"So Gaeetan? How old would you say he is?" I stop at the fireplace and sit at the table's head.

"Do not do this, Natalia. It is not wise to look for answers that hold no weight on our lives."

"Oh, but do they not?" I pour myself a glass of wine, tempted by the rise in the room's temperature. "You yourself said that Gaeetan talked of the blue blood that runs through my veins. You yourself told of stories your great-great-grandfather held about a time of dragons. And is it not also true that this is the one man who has pushed for my death? How I owe it to him? To his people?"

Cyprien stands. Clearing his throat, he brushes his napkin from his lap and clasps his hands behind his back. Moving over to me in gentle glides, he pulls my chair sideways and kneels to face me eye to eye. "And what if it is true, Natalia? What if your life means more to these people once you're dead than when you walk among them?"

Taking a sip from the glass now held in my hands, I laugh. "You forget, Cyprien, that is a truth I have always held."

"Why? Why offer to die for people who hate you? For people who hold you without a future?" His voice remains harsh, his eyes boring into me.

"They do not all hate me."

"All it takes is a few."

"If there is a chance, even the smallest possibility, that my life gives people more hope, more courage, and the façade of guidance, I would do it over and over." I lean my head closer to his. "One life is never worth that of hundreds."

Cyprien takes the wine glass from my hands and gulps it down. He places the glass on the table and stands to face the fire.

"Gaeetan never intended for a marriage. He hates me because of choices long gone from his grasp," I say. "He never anticipated the prophecy would reach its conclusion the way it was originally prophesized. Whether I die today or die tomorrow remains irrelevant to him." Refilling the empty glass, I drink the red liquid in one swift movement.

"And what is accomplished if you were to die?" he says.

"Hope. My death gives them hope."

"You're wrong, Natalia. Your death gives an old man revenge and another reason to reign over people he no longer cares for. His pride is the only thing it saves. Your death will be meaningless!" His voice rises.

"It's all I have left!" I scream.

I stand to leave.

Cyprien reaches out and grabs my wrist. His eyes hold darkness, but his stance is beaten and fatigued from years of sorrow hanging on his shoulders. "There is a tunnel in the hall to his chambers. The guards rotate at dusk. Find the stone with the edge smooth as the sand."

Letting go of my wrist, he stalks out of the dining hall, taking the bottle of wine with him.

Chapter Thirty-Nine
Quinn

"How can I convince you to turn back and wait this out?" Bailey says before dusk hits their cabin.

"You can't. And honestly, you wouldn't want to." Quinn stuffs clothes into his pack. "You pretend you don't want me involved, but we both know you have begged me to stay at your side since mom died."

"This is different, Quinn. It's not an illness. It's a war."

"And it wasn't a vacation either. It wasn't a park or a freakin playdate. It was an excavation. It all started with an excavation." Quinn stuffs his toothbrush into his mouth as he talks. "All the reasons are moot. It's happening."

"You are both talking nonsense," Ryan says. "You're both doing it, you're both going along with it, and the only reason you're arguing about it is because it makes you feel better."

"How on earth would arguing with Pops here make me feel better?" Quinn says after spitting out a mouth full of water.

"Because otherwise you have to stop and think about what's really at stake, and that reason is the only thing that is different for both of you."

"It's the same reason," Bailey says.

"No, it's not." Ryan points a finger at Bailey. "It's the life a child. A child you are treating like your own. And it's friendship. One built on trust that she has always held in you." He points his other finger at Quinn. "A trust you will do anything to keep. God knows why. Before she showed up all you ever did was bitch and moan."

Quinn wrinkles his nose. "I take offense to that. I'd like to think that my bitching and moaning hasn't ceased one bit, thank you very much."

Bailey slouches on his cot. "So, what's it to you?"

The air is full of moisture from the river and smells from the fire. Ryan's silence softens the space in the small cabin, and he shrugs. "It's family."

Ryan has been family for as long as Quinn can remember. A kinship that has grown through the years and rested on his shoulders without weight. Whenever Ryan left them, it was only for a few weeks at a time. Then he would find his way back to Bailey and follow along with whatever scheme or dig Bailey had planned, stepping up to the plate whenever Quinn needed a brother instead of a father.

Maybe the same was for Natalia. If only it hadn't been so easy for her to walk away. As they plan their route and defenses with a clan of people hidden from the ages of time, she is lost to him in a jungle not so far away.

They organize men, practice battle techniques, and sharpen weaponry. His body falls into bed each night aching not only from the fatigue, but also the panic. Panic that her choices have already been made, that they don't get to her in time, or that she won't be as happy to see him as he will her.

If she has wed, may it not be for death. If she was found, may it not have been by the Iritans.

"How do we know these Iritans don't have technology or weaponry like the rest of the world?" Quinn pulls his sleeping bag to his shoulders as he eyes the open window. "Kinodans are hidden from the world and locked in time. We stand no chance with blades if we're attacked with bombs."

"We have to trust that Iritan is locked in time, too. They are still clinging to the hopes of a blood sacrifice to save their people, for crying out loud," Ryan says. "If they have bombs, would taking Natalia's life be necessary?"

"Bombs, huh?" Both men turn to stare at Quinn with accusation in their eyes.

"Are you suggesting we bring bombs to the party?" Bailey says.

Quinn shrugs. "I'm just saying, with the right materials I can make it happen."

Bailey's eyebrows rise halfway up his brow, and his neck tilts as he shakes his head.

"What? Unlike the poor folks living here in the stone age, I actually grew up with the internet."

"Medieval times. Probably closer to the Medieval ages," Bailey says.

"If I had an education, I would have known that," he says.

Bailey folds himself into his sleeping bag. "Think of me as your personal educator. Now, go to bed. We'll ask around tomorrow. See if we can find the ingredients for your so-called bombs."

"Are we really thinking of bombing people for her?" Ryan says.

"Yes," Bailey and Quinn say in unison.

Even if he can't make a bomb, he can do better than sharpened swords and hatchets. Maybe some good old-fashioned fire balls.

If only he could muster up a dragon.

Chapter Forty
Natalia

I don't sleep. I pace my room as I wait. For hours. I wait by the cracks in my door for dusk to hit. Just as Cyprien said, the guard walks away from my door at dusk.

Cracking the door as slowly as I can, I tiptoe down the hall. Arriving at Gaeetan's unguarded door, I slide my hands over the coarse stones. Sweat drips down my brow, and I push away the panic. My time is running out. I step back and focus on the edges of each stone. Gliding my thumbs across one stone at a time, I finally find a smoothed edge just below eye level.

I push the stone in and hear the faintest of clicks. The wall of stone moves and opens into a dark chamber. Slipping inside the passageway, I urge the wall to close as Cyprien rounds the corner.

He is in night clothes, striding down the hall to Gaeetan's rooms at a casual pace. His face holds no expression, but his eyes are fixed on me. He stops in front of me. He says nothing but touches the same stone that led me entry into the tunnel.

The wall closes between us, and I am left standing in an unknown corridor, leaving Cyprien to wait on the other side of the wall of stone.

My breath quickens at first, but once my eyes adjust to the darkness, I can make out a faint light at the bottom of a circular stairway.

A part of me fears I was tricked to my doom, locked away in the depths of a castle to suffocate or starve. Cyprien never held much stock in my prophecy. How hard would it be to hide me just to anger Gaeetan? Perhaps he will kill me in secret now that I hold the will of the people. He may succumb to Gaeetan's wishes and commands, but he struggles with his devotion. Relation is the only thing that ties Cyprien to Gaeetan. Not care or concern. Although appearances speak otherwise, I doubt his dedication. Does he stay with Gaeetan out of fear or because he knows no different?

Taking one step at a time, I stumble down a series of steps, my hands flat against the cold wall for balance. I gag at the smell of sulfur, a rotten odor that tugs at my insides and begs me to turn back.

I cover my mouth and pinch the smells away the best I can. At the bottom of the staircase, I find more light. Water coats the walls and collects on the cold floor. My feet stamp in puddles, no longer trying to be quiet.

The tunnel opens into a cave and a pain hits my heart so sharply it seeps out my mouth in a whimper and a gasp.

The dragon that lies in the middle of the floor is in shackles. The chains around its neck are so large I could slip through undetected. The pathetic creature only moves its eyes at the sight of me, and a small puff of smoke flows out of its nostrils, nothing more.

The dragon's muscles have withered during his confinement. Wrinkly skin and fleshy scabs cover the lower half of the dragon, but its scales are missing.

I approach, my heart skipping and my hands shivering. I reach for the dragon, but it does not move. I touch the burdened shoulder of the injured creature.

"You are not the same dragon I once knew," I whisper.

The scales left in place are moist, held with very little residue and dust that I had come to know while in my own cave. The blue scales have more green than gray in them. Long ago, residue would wash onto my skin at each touch, like soot from a fire, leaving blue shimmers on my skin. The scales I touch now barely have a shine at all.

"I had a dragon keeper once," I whisper. "Oh, how I had hated him at first." I drop my hands from his skin and sit close to the dragon's head. With my legs crossed, and my arms wrapped around my knees, I only consider for the briefest of moments that this dragon could boil my blood if it desired.

Close enough to touch his nostrils, but far enough that both eyes are in view. I drop my head in mourning. "I am so sorry. I, too, was trapped in a cave. Although I had no chains holding me in place, it felt as though I had."

I lift my head to meet his gaze, tormented by the rise and fall of my own chest. "But unlike yourself, I was safe, and I was cared for greatly."

The dragon drops its head to the ground at this, as if it took too much energy to focus on me.

"We are better than this, aren't we?"

I rise from my seat to touch its snout. It exhales, breath warmer than the surrounding humidity. "It has only been recently that my chains became real. Yours ... it seems have been here for quite some time."

I walk around the dragon's neck and fumble with its chains. "I suppose there is a key?"

Without finding a key, but a mechanism holding a lock sternly in place, I return to meet his gaze.

"Will you trust me?" I whisper.

The dragon's eyes blink and rest on me for only a moment. The rise and fall of its head is so feeble I fear I could have missed it.

"I will find your key and get you out."

I straighten the folds on my dress and stand tall. "Together. Together we will free our chains."

Chapter Forty-One
Quinn

They leave at the first quarter moon. They take turns with the alpacas, guiding their belongings around the mountain, only to face two more slopes at its rear. With the air cooler in the day, they find it much easier to travel longer distances without waiting for the cover of night.

The mountain is rumbling at all hours of the day and the steam lashes out from its core.

Quinn didn't know active volcanoes existed in these parts. He thought the one semiology chart found back at the villa had been a fluke, and their actual arrival at Kinoda still left him dumbfounded. When he had pointed to the Kinoda on the map, it had been a mere guess.

He had never been a decent navigator. When his father told him to take a right, he would turn so hard it was nearly a left. When asked to make a circle around a camp, he would have to backtrack in the woods several times before his circle matched that of his father's expectations.

Finding Kinoda had been a stroke of luck, yet his father still regarded him with pride for it. Kinodans puzzle Quinn. Although a people of great tradition with legends held high, they throw themselves into the fight quicker than he would have imagined. He expected that of Iritans. They represent a darkness Natalia's father refused to send her to. He expected a quieter disposition from the Kinodans. Nevertheless, they dropped their gathering ways, put ashes on their fires, and closed up their minds to anything other than fighting for their queen's return.

Although the women stay behind, they urge the men on and scream of revenge and unworthy alliances. The children skip behind them as they leave.

Maybe that was what went wrong in the first place. Both groups of people got so clouded with the past they forgot what was truly at stake. A girl was to sacrifice her life in trade for a peace treaty. Her life. For peace.

But peace is hard to come by when both sides are so hungry for war.

He tries to explain his thoughts to Bailey. To Ryan. But beneath all his ideas he can't find answers to an underlying question. What if they are too late?

"We try and talk to the tribe leader," Bailey says. "We can't just go in there with swords raised. Natalia and countless other innocents will suffer and die if we do."

"We might need to convince her to leave," Ryan says. "Starting a war at her feet might not be the best way to accomplish that."

"I guess it's a good thing the bombs are at the back of the caravan then," Quinn says.

"We have a two-day hike left in us. Two days to figure it out before all hell breaks loose."

Bailey is right, but Quinn can't shake the worry in his gut. What if they don't succeed? What if they don't get to her in time?

He cups his hand around the remnants of the dragon scale and prays for reassurance.

Chapter Forty-Two
Natalia

Cyprien waits for me outside the tunnels. He convinces his guards he wants to hold watch over Gaeetan because the crazy old man wants to slit my throat in my sleep. As prince of the tribe, he cannot let that happen.

Cyprien's eyes flash, pained and humbled. "Make way to your quarters. Say nothing to the guard at your door. We will use it to our advantage."

Without asking questions, I nod and follow his orders. My feet tangle in my robes as I hurry down the hallway. I slow once I turn the corner.

The guard gapes at me. "Were you not in your room?"

"No. I was not." I push past him and opens the door to my chambers. As I close the door, the guard hurries away, most likely to rat me out to Cyprien. I hope it is Cyprien at least.

My head hits the pillow and for the first time since I lost poor Santino, a blanket of deep despair surrounds me. For the first time in a long time, I question my purpose. I reach behind my neck and pull off the chestnut necklace. I stare at the ceiling and imagine a heaven like Quinn's where his mother looks down on him and guides him.

I envision a young woman cradling an infant wrapped in cloth. Nursing him when he wakes in the night, holding him up in the light of the day, and watching as the sun blesses his skin.

My mother did no such things. My mother's life bled out at my birth, and yet my people still perished. Sacrifice or not, my people died one by one. Time halted nothing. For what is prosperity really? Is it keeping people from war? Punishing men in chains when there is no other to punish? Or is it the blessing of that sunlight on a babe's skin? The chance that a mother looks down on her young ones, guiding them as they falter?

My father was my guide. From the trials of pampering a young girl to meet a king or being pulled from the village streets to be raised in seclusion, he was always there to give me strength. Even as my life should have ended in death, oh so long ago, he was my strength.

I imagine a mother would hold the same devotion to a child.

"Guide me, my mother," I whisper into the darkness of my room. "You gave your people your life. Please. Please give me your guidance."

I push away the tears rolling down my face when a knock shakes my door. I adjust her robes and try to flatten the untamed hair on my shoulders.

I open the door. Cyprien waits with two guards, his checks drawn, his shoulders pulled back and an oil lamp in his hand.

"May I enter?" he says.

A slight nod of my head and he enters my chambers and closes the door behind him. He leaves both guards outside the door.

He paces the room with soft and measured strides. He paces in his night clothes, still perfectly pressed to match the blue in his hair.

I sit on the edge of my bed. My hands grasp the bed comforter. "Does the blue in your hair come from the dragons?"

"No, my dear. That would be modern hair dye." He sits in the chair nestled under the window, the night still holding high. "I find it ironic."

"Hideously distasteful, Cyprien. That dragon is dying at our feet."

"Yes, I fear it is. Gaeetan has made sure of that." He rests his forehead on his hand, the open palm cupping the skin under his hair.

"Have you even seen it lately? Do you have any idea how badly he fares?"

"No. I fear my cowardice keeps me from him."

"I should let him burn you to a crisp!" I say.

His eyes soften. "My my, you think me awful. Regardless of what you may think, I do not fear the dragon. I fear what has happened to him. Worse still, I fear what will become of him."

"I made it a promise," I whisper.

His eyes dart up, and he stands. He moves with grace and sits on the bed next to me. My body heat rises at his nearness. Unclenching my fingers from the grasp of the blanket, he takes my hand into his own. "And how to you plan on making that promise?"

"I haven't quite figured that out yet."

"I might have a plan to help, but I fear you might not like it." He says.

"If it sets this world straight, any option is better than none." I say.

"Marry me, Natalia. Not because of some promised sacrifice or agreement made centuries ago. Marry me because I am me and you are you." His thumb rubs against the softness of my skin, and my insides tremble. "Together we will change the skies. We will see Gaeetan's reign come to an end. We will create the empire of your dreams. I will give you an empire free of chains, Natalia."

"Even for the dragons?" I say.

"We will need to get Gaeetan out of the way first. As long as he is around, I cannot touch the dragon."

"I am not a murderer, Cyprien."

"But he is, Natalia."

"There are so many things I wish to understand. Things from then. Things from now."

"I do not hold all of the answers you seek, but I do hold a future."

He drops to his knees, his eyes closing as he rests my hands on his knees. "Take your time and think it through. I trust you will let me know when you make a decision." He kisses the back of my hand as he stands, then bows his head and takes his leave.

I fall asleep pondering his pledge, the possibility of a marriage without the promise of a sacrifice attached. Although his ideas of an empire are a bit naïve, I can't help but presume that his notions might hold weight for the farmers of the land. But what of the guards? Where will their loyalties lie without the influence of Gaeetan?

With my own emotions and longings put aside, my cheeks flush and I clasp hope once more.

Quinn climbs the trees as instructed and gropes his way to the tallest vantage point. His eyes remain on Bailey as Ryan's remain on Quinn. One man in front of the other, the lineup of warriors follows a mile out, surrounding the territory in a semicircle. With little training in battle, they focus on isolating the Iritans. If a runner is needed to get through the lines, a message could be passed on like a telephone.

They are approaching the mountain's base and the plan's outcome rests heavily on Bailey's shoulders. He will approach first. He will be the one to try and talk some sense into her first.

Up in the trees, Quinn sees the entrance to the stone castle clear enough through the thin foliage. He waits in the trees for Bailey's entrance to the castle. His heart jumps as he sees two figures exit the stone archway.

She wears white. The gown stops at her calves to expose the black leather of her boots. The linen flows from her bodice and cups her shoulders as it trails down her sides. Her hair is pulled out of her face, the curls tamed peacefully on top of her head.

She holds the hand of the man next to her. His black hair glimmers blue at the tips. He does not wear linen like the people he faces. He wears jeans, much like the ones Quinn wears. His white button-down shirt matches Natalia's gown.

He cannot hear what is said by the man, but as their clasped hands reach to the sky, the crowd of hundreds erupts in applause. His heart breaks to see her holding another's hand.

The crowd slowly begins to part as Bailey makes his way through the populace. Like a snake through a field of grass, his path is persistent and true. By the time Bailey enters the open dome, his gait is slow but confident. It is the walk Quinn has known since a child. He has always wished he could hold his shoulders as high and master his father's gait.

Two uniformed men take Bailey to Natalia and the Prince of Iritan. Natalia drops the prince's hand and runs to Bailey. Her arms wrap around his neck and Bailey's arms encircle her waist.

He sees their embrace, her hold on him as strong as the beat of his pulse.

A conversation commences. Natalia steps back and allows Bailey to hold much of his conversation with the movement of his hands.

She doesn't take her eyes off Bailey, but the men around her grow anxious. Even Cyprien begins to pace behind her.

But Bailey does not let their anxiety take away from their reunion. His eyes are only on Natalia, and his words of truth lie at her feet.

Chapter Forty-Four
Natalia

"Mr. Bailey!"

Joy rises in my throat, too proud of the man who found his way to me. Too proud to consider his reasons.

"How are you, my dear girl?"

Resting his palms on her shoulders, he pushes her back slightly to get a good look at her. His eyes are watery with what I can only assumes is concern.

"I am very well. There is no need to fret. I have missed you so."

My eyes search his, and for a moment I am reminded that two guards ushered him in. And I am also reminded of the reason I left his side in the first place. He should not be here.

"I have missed you, too, my girl. We have been worried sick."

My eyes search behind him for Ryan and Quinn. "Did you come alone?"

"No, Natalia. I have come with hundreds. Hundreds who have come for you."

Hundreds. He came with hundreds. Does that mean Quinn and Ryan are safe? Does that mean he kept enough sense to make them hold their distance?

Gaeetan approaches from behind me, the small drag of his cane over the dirt giving him away. The shuffle of his feet erases the sounds of Kinodan hope. Hope drawn on cave walls. Hope placed in Mr. Bailey and Mr. Bailey alone.

My head turns toward the castle as Gaeetan storms up. His hair is as black as night by the fires of Estancia. Black hate illuminates from his skin.

He seethes his hatred as Bailey speaks the Kinodan name once more. His eyes flash against the darkest of all my memories, a hatred so deep it forms knots in my stomach. Beyond the darkness of the cave, or the tears I shed at night, I see the king of my childhood. A man I had to strain my neck to look up to, and who cursed the gold he would trade for my life. He never wanted to treaty. He just wanted the girl. This is the man who took me from my father.

Chapter Forty-Five
Quinn

The old man's shoulder nudges past the prince and pushes Natalia out of his way.

Quinn sees the glimmer of the blade from his vantage point in the trees, but his brain does not acknowledge the silver in time. His screams erupt as Gaeetan pushes his body and the blade into Bailey, the pressure pushing against Quinn's heart.

The echoes from the trees cry with Quinn as Bailey crumbles onto the ground.

Chapter Forty-Six
Natalia

I do not breathe. I cannot breathe. My breath leaves me as screams erupt in the forest. my heart stops, my mind shuts down.

I hover over the limp body on the ground, my face striped with tears. Cyprien is yelling, and Gaeetan is laughing at his rear, but I block everything. Cyprien's rage. Gaeetan's evil. All the people swarming into the arena. I even block out the war erupting all around me. The pain and the nausea in my gut are all that hold me in place.

I try to stem the flow of blood out of Bailey's stomach wound. He is awake and tries to shush my tears. Quinn arrives from nowhere. His face pale, his life seems to be escaping me just as quickly as Mr. Baileys. My face begs his forgiveness as he kneels beside his father, the blue absent from his eyes.

"It's okay, Pops, it's okay."

"I told you swords would lead to trouble," Bailey whispers.

"You are going to be just fine. We are going to get you out of here. Out of *this*, and you are going to be just fine." Quinn can barely keep the tremors out of his voice.

Bailey grabs the back of Quinn's neck. Blood drips from his hands. He wipes the tears that fall from Quinn's face. His chest heaves, and he gasps for air that will not come. "You've always been *my* chestnut."

"Quinn…" I whisper but hold onto Bailey's face as the life slowly drains from his body. "Quinn, give me the dragon's scale."

Quinn's eyes dart to Natalia. "No…"

"He needs it, Quinn. Please. You must hurry."

He pulls the dusty blue remnant of the scale from his back pocket. I take what is left from my Keeper out of Quinn's hand for I fear it is our only choice. The blood covering my hands hides the magnificence of it. "Hold it in your mouth, Mr. Bailey."

"Dad…"

Bailey opens his mouth and closes it around the scale. His eyes pull toward Quinn one last time, and he nods at his son.

As Bailey's eyes close, Quinn lets out a horrified scream that reverberates on the mountain.

An explosion shakes the ground.

As I cry and Quinn screams, spears fly over our heads.

I reach for him and tries to calm the storm raging in his chest. Maybe in easing his pain, some of my own pain would subside.

I am not sure of when the war commenced around me. Or how the farmers I tried so long, so desperately to protect, now fight next to the same men who beat and tortured them. The men they fight are the Kinodans who must have come with Bailey.

Men fall all around me. Dying for me. Bleeding for me. Women scramble away from the weapons and run their children into the sanctuary of the woods.

The clang of metal against metal echoes in my soul. It is the sound these people have yearned for centuries. They merely halted at my absence, but this war never truly ended.

Whether it be about land, or gold, or glory, the reasons were lost in time. This is what I was supposed to die for, to end this madness once and for all.

I stand while wiping my hands down the side of my face, wet with a mixture of blood and tears. I wander through the destruction and drop to her knees in front of the castle.

The war does not fight over my head but all around me. It surrounds the castle and the mountain. The men from the east and from the west. It is everywhere. Death lies everywhere.

Silence folds into me as I kneel in front of the dark fortress. Consumed with frustration. Ignited by disappointment, my mind fails to notice the change. The fighting comes to a halt, and the only sound is Gaeetan's maniacal laughter with the dragon at his back, sickly, weak, and lethargic. But it holds the attention of every fighter in the arena. Iritan and Kinoda alike pause at the sight of the dragon. Its giant torso hovers over the stone mountain. The chains that hold its neck wrap around Gaeetan's arms, but he maintains control only because the dragon is so weak.

"Come now, everyone. Let the fighting subside. Let us gather as one." Grabbing Cyprien by the shoulders with his free hand, Gaeetan squeezes.

Hate pours out of Cyprien's glare.

People stare in confusion, their weapons merely paused mid stride.

"Are we not all here for the unity of two people? Kinoda and Iritan alike? Let's end this war once and all. Please! Let's dine!"

"Are you mad?" Cyprien whispers.

Gaeetan points to me. "This one first! She is what has brought our two peoples together today, is she not?"

"Gaeetan…." Cyprien rests on his knees, his shirt now covered in blood.

Gaeetan raises his arms. "Now!"

His shouts make the dragon squirm; its scales stand up like the fur on a frightened cat. Even with few scales left, the dragon's body is an armor not only shielding Gaeetan as its master, but the demands he makes. It fills the arena with fear.

Quinn is hauled to his feet as weapons are dropped to the ground. His arms are pulled back, though he fights to stay on the ground next to his father. It takes two men and a fist to his gut to drag him off the ground and to the stone castle. He ignores the dragon and keeps his eyes on the blood stained on shirt, a sure reminder of the blade thrust into Bailey's gut.

I, too, am pulled to my feet. But the comprehension of it fills like a nightmare that won't seem to stop.

Hundreds of people fill the arena and circle around the dragon chained to the center. Blood covers some, while others wear only sweat and dirt. All show unease and dread. But as the guards follow Gaeetan inside the castle, others follow them. And one by one, the arena empties of Iritan and Kinodan alike.

I wait until the last moment, shocked at how many follow the evil man and his tortured pet. They should know better. Each and every one. Eventually, I am pushed inside, but my eyes turn back. Ryan hovers over Bailey's lifeless body, and I feel the hatred grow inside me. My sadness turns to rage and fury.

I push towards Quinn, him following the crowd like the walking dead. I squeeze Quinn's hand and urge his broken spirit to wake up.

Chapter Forty-Seven
Quinn

He holds no recollection of how he entered the massive hall, or how the people filled the hall so quickly. Hundreds upon hundreds.

Silence envelops the crowd. Fear. Shame. Death. Weariness. It all bears down on them. It all bears down on him. The emptiness in their eyes mirrors that of his own. Even the prince holds emptiness in his eyes. For it was a single man, one evil man who took the life of his father. Defenseless, his father had tried to make simple terms of peace. He aimed to speak to Natalia's heart and convince her to come home. And now he was gone, killed by an old man holding the leash to a dragon as if it were a dog.

Gaeetan laughs and holds up a cup. "Everyone must drink! Guards! Give these warriors a drink! Let's have a toast!"

"Gaeetan…" Cyprien's pleas are weak, the emotion striped from his voice.

"EVERYONE MUST DRINK!"

His echoes fill the hall as the earth quakes. Their feet tremble, and they fear it is the old man's will under their toes. Silence and fear bounce off people seated at tables, slouched against the frames of the wall, or hovering against the window arches.

The unstable shouts from the old man demand to be heard. To

be followed. Hundreds of eyes are glued on him. His eyes glow with crazed desire as he stands in front of the massive fireplace.

"You too, you fools! Make sure to save some for yourselves!" Even the demands placed on his guards are terrifying.

One by one wine glasses are passed out. People take it with apprehension. Confusion. Relief in the face of death.

The old man's raging blaze is much like the rage in Quinn's soul.

Bailey once told him that silence tells the true message from within. That if you listen close enough, you will hear more than words could ever tell. He listens to the silence of hundreds as everyone is served a glass of wine. Even the staff holds the wine in their hands as the masses wait to toast. Silence is strained with fear throughout the hall.

He is pushed into a seat beside Natalia and Cyprien. She no longer holds the prince's hand; instead, her hand grasps his. Her hold is tight, urgent, and filled with something he has not yet seen in her.

"Not them." Gaeetan scowls. "These three do not deserve to drink."

No glasses sit at their table, nor are they offered one.

"Iritan! Kinoda! Let us drink! Let us toast Natalia of Estancia, the fair maiden who has at last brought our people together!" Gaeetan sips his wine as his eyes scan the massive room. His eyes pierce those of even his own guards.

People are crammed in the hall so tightly their questioning looks fall like dominoes. But they hesitate. While some sip their toast, like machines too afraid to upset their master, others remain frozen as the statures carved on the castle.

"Perhaps I did not make myself clear." He walks to Aroura, pulling a pistol from the back of his pants. He points the barrel directly into the back of her head. "I said, a toast!"

Gaeetan raised his glass again. "To the girl who brought you death. Hundreds of years ago, as well as the one under your feet here today."

Everyone else takes a drink. Even the guards who hated her at her arrival. Even Horace who couldn't even stand to walk next to her in the halls.

One by one they fall. Glass shatters as it hits the floor. Moans erupt from those watching before they themselves fall. Screams pierce the lips of those left to wait for their own demise. Their bodies hover over each other, their eyes glassy as they close. One by one they fall, death on their poisoned lips as it drips from their glasses.

Natalia's hand falls from Quinn's grasp, and she covers a sob of disbelief. Gaeetan walks himself back to the head of the table.

Cyprien pushes away from her to his feet, his palms pulsing on the table before the laughing old man. "These are your people! What did you do?"

As the guards, too, drop at his side, Gaeetan's laughs ring in Quinn's ears.

"These people are worthless. Pitiful fliers dreaming of worthless dragons."

Gaeetan walks away from the fire's flames and places both hands on Cyprien's shoulders. "I merely gave them their dragon."

His maliciousness hits Cyprien, and he falls back in his chair. Shock whitens his face.

Gaeetan sneers. "You think they admired you? Wanted you as an heir? The young prince who announces his engagement to a girl who races to another with the drop of one man's blood? Please. You have become a fool."

Natalia's hand squeezes Quinn's under the table, her grasp alive, filled with purpose. She squeezes life back into his soul as the shaking in the ground becomes stronger.

The violence of the quake tears mortar off the walls, and cracks the floor where people lie.

Grasping the table with his free hand, Quinn pulls Natalia closer, determined not to lose her too. Not to the earth screaming its rage nor to the crazy old man spewing death like oxygen.

Gaeetan catches the movement and glares at Natalia. "The mountain speaks today. And today the mountain will finally have its sacrifice. It will burn and rumble as it eats you whole, girl. Only then will the mountain's screams subside." His eyes strike Natalia like rocks in an avalanche.

"And what will you do?" Cyprien says. "What will become of you?"

"I will leave with my dragon and find a new people who deserve such a great sacrifice!" He makes his way to the fire and stares into the flames like they are the image he so desires. "I am not just giving the mountain the promised sacrifice of the ages, but hundreds more. My every desire will be granted by the gods."

"And of us?" Cyprien says.

"You can die with the mountain for all I care." Gaeetan spits as he talks, no longer attempting to capture the admiration of a crowd.

He turns to face the table as Cyprien stands, the earth trembling under his feet. Slowly striding toward his grandfather, his head tilts as if pondering the absurdity of his claims, maybe pondering the desire to be at his side as it happens.

"It is too bad my gods are not the same as yours." Cyprien thrusts a knife and pierces Gaeetan's heart. He pulls him closer into the blade with his free hand. He takes hold of the old man's head and whispers in his ear. "The mountain will eat *you* whole and burn your tyranny to the ground."

The old man grimaces as the color drains from his face, and as his final breath escapes his lungs, he says, "Her blood is the only thing that will end the devastation."

His eyes close, and Cyprien lets the old man drop to the floor.

Chapter Forty-Eight
Natalia

"I failed them. I failed all of them."

My shaking fingertips let go of Quinn's hand as I stand to look upon the horror. "I was supposed to save them. All of them. But all I have done is bring them doom."

Cyprien ignores my distress and the chaos in the room. "The volcano is going to explode." He wipes the blood on his hands onto his blood-soaked jeans.

"I am not leaving them, Cyprien!" My high-pitched voice echoes across the hall. "Their death will not be in vain! I need to be here for them! I need to be here with them!"

"There is nothing you can do! They are dead!" Pointing to the dead man at his feet, Cyprien's voice becomes soft. "Their lives ended because of him, as will ours if we don't get out of the mountain's path before it's too late."

Tears stream down my face as I slump in the chair. I refuse to succumb to fear of the tremoring ground.

The smell of sulfur fills the room. Pulling the top of my dress over my mouth, I struggle to breathe fresh air. The temperature rises as heat fills the room and steam pours in through the cracks in the walls.

Quinn stands and moves past me. He wanders the room, then stops and stares at people huddled together on the ground. Even the strongest of the warriors are crumpled on the floor.

He bends down and places a head on one man's chest. "He's still breathing." His eyes flash to Natalia. "It wasn't poison." Picking up one of the broken glasses from the ground, his fingers brush against the liquid. "He mixed scales in with the wine."

"Cyprien, how long will they sleep?" I say. "How long before they wake up?"

"I…I don't know. It depends on the dosage. It could be hours. It could be days."

"We don't have days! The volcano is going to erupt. You said it yourself."

On my feet once more, I bend down next to Quinn and place my open palm on the man's head.

"I don't know how to wake up hundreds of people. Even if we weren't in the volcano's path, we can't stay here. We need to leave." Quinn kneels beside me. "You need to leave before it's too late."

"We need someone to help us!"

Quinn stares at the men he arrived with, men either facing their death as they sleep, or men outside the crumbling castle who will die from the mountain ash or the lava that will soon flow over the ground like currents of blood.

"Natalia, we need to go. I don't, I don't know what else to do," Quinn says.

"No!"

I gaze at the sleeping faces in the room. My eyes do not miss a soul. Not so long ago, these souls fought on different sides. Some I never knew, others I begged pardon for with my life. Will their women be waiting when they don't return home? Will their children remember their fathers like I had? Or will they, too, be swept up with the volcano, destined to perish in its path?

"Darius!" I cry. "Cyprien! Darius isn't in here!"

"Darius?" Quinn says.

Cyprien's eyes graze the room and stop on Quinn. "I will get him. You get her out."

The sob that originates in my chest pleads with the decision my feet make for me. They are right. There is nothing I can do. I shuffle toward the door, a shuffle that pulls like a weight at my ankles. My feet know as just as much as my heart that what we are doing is wrong. Leaving is wrong.

Quinn follows me out of the main hall. I turn my head to see Cyprien race down the hall in the other direction.

As we exit the stone pillars of the main hall, the scene developing before us only confirming our original suspicions. We don't have much time.

Grey snowflakes fall from the sky and make the mountain's intent known. The ground is covered in ash, from the stone pillars at the entrance to the paths leading to the farms. Even the trees have ash hanging from the branches like icicles.

The dragon glowers at them and blocks the arena's exits. Cinders cover its bare skin and mask his missing scales. Its energy has returned with the death of Gaeetan, and it stands tall and wide, facing a battle for the first time since making my acquaintance.

Whipping the chains around its neck, the dragon lashes at its place in the middle of the open dome. Surrounded by mounds of volcanic ash, it steps over the war's dead. Its teeth grind at the anger covering it like blood on a knife, and smoke billows from its nostrils.

My arms wave at Quinn, trying to get his attentions through the thick ash falling from the sky. "Get its chains!"

Quinn heads for the dragon's collar, and the dragon slows. He drops its head to the ground and remains still. Only its eyes blink as he waits.

Quinn picks up the keys dropped at the dragon's feet and slowly approaches the angry yet somber dragon. Fear is evident on its face and by the tension in its body. Quinn is careful not to touch the beast as the chains clatter to the ground, then he retreats to stand beside me, just as Cyprien and Darius exit the castle.

His face is still bruised and confused panic rests on his shoulders, but Darius is alive. Quinn playfully punches him on the shoulder, and they both embrace. The stone behind them crumbles and cracks as the ground shakes. The earth screams that it is time for them to make their leave.

"Let's get out of here," Darius says as he looks Quinn up and down.

The dragon curls its talons into the dirt and ash. Its muscles, though withered, hold stronger than the stone at the base. The shaking stops, but the dragon remains in place. Neither the quieting rumble of the earth nor the four of them entice the dragon to move. But it does bare its fangs and growls a warning. Not to the mountain, not to the captors who held it captive, not even to the chains. But to me.

I point to the sky and the forest. "You need to leave. *We* need to leave."

Yet the dragon does not move. It remains firm, guarding the path into the forest and escape, growling, and breathing smoke from its nostrils.

"Go!" I shout. "You must leave this place."

I approach the dragon. "Take your freedom and leave!" Pointing toward the sky once more I signal to it, my fear no longer for myself, but for it. What would happen if it too stayed?

Without losing another moment, I motion to my companions and head for the forest, farther and farther from the death at my heels.

But the dragon will have none of it. It moves to block me from leaving. Guarding my path, it pushes its snout at me and knocks me to the ground.

"We are going to die! We must leave!"

I climb to my feet, my hands now gray at my sides. Gripping my boots in the dust, I ready myself.

Its snout nudges me once more, pushing me closer to the stone entrance.

Quinn, Darius, and Cyprien stumble out of the way, all frightened by the dragon's actions.

"What do you want me to do?" I say as my rear soaks up the dirt and ash from the ground.

Its snout motions to the stone castle. Its growl heaves in the air, and it lies flat on the ground below the steps in front of me. We stand trapped against the castle, trapped by a fire-breathing dragon growling like a bully.

"I can't save them!" I say. "I can do no more here!"

The dragon stops snarling and reaches for me as the ash falls from the sky. Tilting its head to the side, its bulbous eyes meet mine. I understand just as its talon pulls down the length of my shoulder.

A few drops of blood drip from the tiny scratch. The dragon motions toward the castle once more.

"It's my blood," I whisper. "My blood is going to save them."

Chapter Forty-Nine
Quinn

He follows her through the entrance and down the hall, hastening to keep up, to keep her from more irrational, poor choices. "Natalia, this is absurd!"

"It's not absurd!"

Stopping in her tracks, she turns and nearly knocks him off his feet. She grabs hold of his hands as her eyes search his. "Quinn, this is the prophecy."

His voice shakes and he is terrified his words will hit her more than he intends while silently pleading that they do. "Natalia, prophecies aren't real."

Her hands drop his like they are burning the softness of her heart. She turns her back on him in one swift movement. "Like dragons, Quinn? Like the blue that runs through my blood? None of these things are real!"

His silence tears at his gut. She believes her truths just as much as the uncertain circumstances that have faced her since the moment they met. Since hundreds of years before they met, in fact. "I don't believe your future has already been predicted, Natalia. I believe your own free will can take you where you want to go."

Her hands reach up to cover her face, and her shoulders droop.

Cyprien approaches her. "Natalia, maybe he is right."

She avoids his gaze.

"Maybe it was just a story. A story a crazy old man told to secure himself a beautiful young bride."

"That means it was all for nothing."

Raising her voice, she turns to face both of them, her cheeks flushed, her tortured eyes damp. "My childhood was taken from me. My mother was taken from me. My father hid me in a cave. Even Santino, poor sweet Santino...." The tears spill over her cheeks. "And you Darius! And Mr. Bailey." Dropping her chin, she wipes her face. "It wasn't for nothing; it couldn't have been all for nothing."

"I am fine, Natalia. Standing right here in front of you, strong as ever." Darius says.

"And Pops wasn't for nothing." Quinn's voice quakes as he lifts her chin up with his forefingers. "What Bailey did was for you."

"Don't you see, Quinn?" She takes his fingers in hers. "That only works if I have a purpose."

"Your purpose has never been death," Cyprien says. He shuffles his feet in the ash. "A savior maybe, but not death."

"But the prophecy was of my death." Taking a step back, she gestures to the large room. "The spill of my blood dripped on each soldier meant to protect them from conquest. It would unite Kinoda and Iritan alike." Her eyes soften as she faces Quinn. "Don't you see? It is the mountain they will face in conquest." She drops her voice, and her turmoil hardens into determination. "I will die trying to protect them. All of them."

"How?" Quinn's whisper breaks in his chest. He fears her resolve but is lost in her hope.

"Easy." Her eyes dart to the massive hall filled with dying

soldiers, farmers, and villagers. Iritans and Kinodans. "I spill my blood, and we drip it on each and every man in that room."

Hearing her words, Quinn pauses to listen to the silence that follows. His choices are limited. She is determined.

The floor begins to shake once more, reminding him their time is near. Not only can he feel it in the ground, but he hears it in the rumble of the earth.

He nods at her slightly and does the same to Darius and Cyprien.

She smiles at him. Taking a deep breath, he feels the air stick to his lungs, thick with gases that don't belong. Cyprien and Darius follow as they make their way into the hall.

At the room's entrance, she picks up the nearest blade and slits her wrist. With no pause, or second thought, she swipes down the length of her vein. The blue shimmer seeps through the red at her wrists, a steady flow.

"Shit, Natalia, maybe some freaking warning," Quinn says.

Racing for the nearest goblet on the floor, he presses its rim against her vein. The blood pours into the glass like water from a fountain, yet her resolve remains firm, and she makes no sound. Her eyes do not glance at the liquid, nor do they consider the ramifications of her actions. They merely hold on Quinn and force him to pretend he calm in the storm.

He passes the filled chalice to Cyprien and nods as he is handed a fresh glass. Once the second is filled, she nods to him as well, silently asking him to follow Cyprien.

Handing her a third goblet, he takes the filled glass and follows Cyprien to the bodies lying on the floor. Dropping his index finger into the cup, he lets his skin caress the shimmering liquid. One drop at a time, he lets it drip into the mouths of the men at his feet.

He is not sure how long they work, or even how to keep track of the men he reached or the men he has yet to help, but he is fully cognizant of the silence the room holds. Hours maybe, enough that the ache in his stomach turns to pain, and his eyelids grow heavy. But he is aware when Cyprien approaches Natalia to refill his cup, a look of uncertainty and a question of permission in his eyes.

He continues to drop her blood on the lips of her people, both fighting for her on opposite sides of the mountain. Although for different reasons, the intent of each was the same. Even if he himself pondered the prophecy, these people certainly did not.

When half the room had been touched, the men on the floor start to stir, and Cyprien, too, approaches Natalia for a new glass, a smile lingering on his lips. It is only then that he notices the color has faded from her skin and her lips are brushed with pink instead of their blood lust red. Her eyes are glassy and her fingers tremble.

She had ripped off her skirt to wrap the wound on her right arm. Tied tight, it takes all the color from her skin.

Quinn grabs at her as she slices a new vein on her opposite arm. "It is enough. We have enough."

She grabs his wrist and holds him steady with her eyes, forcing his hand to collect the newly dripping blood at her wrist. She pleads with him. "No, it is not enough." Her voice cracks.

"There are enough men who stir. They will wake and help get the other men out."

Cyprien and Darius approach at his words, their lips tight. Following their stare, Quinn looks at Natalia's fresh wound. Her blood dribbles into the glass like lava. Thick. Slow. Red.

"I'm sure it's fine," he says. But even at his words, Natalia's eyelids close, and she collapses to the floor.

Quinn grabs her as she falls.

"I'm sure it's fine, she is going to be fine." Cyprien's eyes sweep the room. "And like you said. The men waking up can help. Darius can help."

Grasping at her dress, he rips off another piece of fabric and tightens it around her open wound. His fingers push into her skin with enough pressure to stop the bleeding. His eyes sweep the room once more. There are too many. There are too many for just two.

The fear locked in his jaw claims his unease, but the quake that hits their feet creates a much more vibrant terror. The ground shakes harder than the temper of the dragon.

The floor cracks in half and pulls chunks of stone off the walls.

"Get her out of here!" Cyprien says. His screams rise above the cracking earth.

The cracks widen and threaten to take the awakening men. "We will get the rest. Get her out of here!"

Quinn staggers to his feet and holds onto Natalia just as much as the floor for support. He cradles her like an infant in his arms and races out of the castle. He leaves both Darius and Cyprien behind.

The dragon is gone by the time he races down the steps. Even his footprints and the chains that once held his neck are invisible under the layers of ash covering the ground like snow.

Quinn races out of the arena, past the trees he hung from a lifetime ago. He is not sure which way he goes. He only hopes that he is moving away from Kinoda. By foot, the distance is too great to get her away from the volcano's torment in time. His only hope is to find a road. Maybe a village. Something. Anything to help save the life of the girl in his arms.

Minutes pass before the shaking subsides, though tremors still vibrate under his toes. The sun moves in the sky, barely visible under the cloak of darkness left by the volcano.

Quinn's movements slow. His arms ache like fire. His legs are jelly under his cramping torso. He stumbles and falls to the ground with a crash. Pulling her higher in his arms to shield her from the fall, his right knee smashes into the stones on the ground. He feels the blood seep through his pants.

He only allows himself a few minutes' rest, just enough to catch his breath, just enough to gain the strength back in his arms. His pants are torn and blood pours down his shins. He tears at the rocks embedded in his skin. He needs water. He finds leaves filled with water and relishes the liquid pouring down his throat.

Quinn touches the water to Natalia's lips. His fingers find her pulse, hidden under her tender skin. Although weak, it's there. And hope is all he needs. The ash of the ground is now a mere dusting. He must have traveled farther than he thought. But if the volcano explodes, it won't be far enough.

And that is just the volcano. His true worries lie with how much blood Natalia has lost, and how she has fallen unconscious and barely holds onto life. Her blood is now the same color as his.

He shouldn't have let her do it.

He lets out a blood-curdling cry, and the silence of the jungle breaks to accept his screams. Reaching his arms under her, he picks her up once more, but her head drops to rest in the crook of his neck.

She is in his charge now, is his responsibility. His chest rises and falls as he swallows his growing panic. He rises and heads deeper into the jungle.

As the sun begins to set on the horizon, he knows he needs to find shelter. He won't get her any farther until he gives his muscles a rest, but if the mountain explodes in the night, he needs to be on higher ground.

The dragon is flying overhead. His wings, the span of a neighborhood block, spread as he glides above the treetops. It circles overhead and signals to Quinn that it is here for him. Here for her. Slow and patient. A savior of sorts, a guide through the dark day.

He follows the path that the dragon leads. In the thickest of the brush overhead, he fears he has lost sight, only to be reassured when the sound of the flapping resonates in his ear. A powerful soar of its wings and he traps the wind in his glide.

By the time he reaches the cave, the sun is hidden behind the horizon. The dragon soars above its chosen destination like a helicopter hovering in one spot. This will be their shelter.

The dragon makes a final circle overhead, its dark shadow cascading across the sky.

If he had the energy to yell his gratitude he would have, but climbing the small slope of rock piles outside the entrance to the small cave takes all his effort.

Darkness envelops the small cave, yet he cares not. Except, of course, for Natalia. If she awakes after he falls unconscious, he fears paranoia will overtake her.

Pulling flint out of his cargo pocket, he starts a fire, and he discovers a pool of water hidden in the corner of the cave. With Natalia nestled near the fire, her arms holding up her head, he tears at his ripped pants. Making a rag, he peels off the bindings on her arms.

He cleans her wounds through his exhaustion. Through the pain in his joints, his swelling knee, and through the pull of his eyelids to close. Only when he has done all he can and applied fresh bandages does he nestle beside her. Checking her pulse once more, he falls asleep.

Chapter Fifty
Quinn

He feels the volcano erupt before he hears it. His heart stops for a beat. Fear pounds in his chest. He had been expecting an earthquake tremor similar to the ones sporadically occurring over the past few days, but the jolt hits stronger and more intensely than he anticipated.

The blast pulls him up from the floor as if the earth has lost its gravity and pulsates the air before the crack a thousand times louder than any thunder he had ever heard. The sound brings the rocks down in front of the cave, a rumble heavier than a freight train. The entrance collapses in, and dust pushes through the cracks of the cave. The campfire flame extinguishes in moments.

The rumble lasts longer than he expects. His insides jerk up and down with the violent cries from the earth. He pulls his knees to his chest and covers Natalia with his body. His arms act as a shield, his head, a helmet. He holds his embrace for minutes after the movements stop. Forcing himself to breathe, he ignores the pulsing ache in his lungs.

He fumbles through his pockets and searches for his flint. He crawls over Natalia's unconscious body and finds the warm remnants of the fire. His wrist flips the flint back and forth until he smells the smoke.

Flames ignite and he finds the courage to make his way to the collapsed entrance. The cave-in is solid and any effort to escape is futile, but his fingers still grasp for cracks. His eyes turn to Natalia. Her hair spills over her face like a waterfall, but her skin lacks any color.

He screams in frustration, the sound echoing in the cave. He holds onto hope at the base of his thoughts. Hope that she will be alright. Hope that Darius and Cyprien got everyone out of the mountain. He hopes her attempts to save all those people were not in vain.

With his legs still wobbly and his joints still protesting, he stands. His knee throbs, but he walks over to her. He had found her in a cave much like this one. Clinging to life without realizing she had so much of it left in her. He watches the weak rise and fall of her chest in the dim light of the fire, the resolve of her cheeks bearing down on his like a rainstorm. He has failed her.

Dropping to his knees, Quinn lets a tear drop and is grateful no one is there to bear witness. He feels her pulse. It is dangerously slow. He is making the right decision.

He pulls the last of the dragon scale from his pocket. Even in the poor light the blue dust shines even though it is wrinkled. As gently as he can, he opens her mouth and closes the scale inside.

Chapter Fifty-One
Quinn

He sleeps through his fatigue. The fire has burned out. When he wakes, the cave is blanketed in pitch black. Not knowing if day or night has taken hold, he doesn't care. He sleeps through more of his exhaustion.

Pangs of hunger wake him time and again. He lets Natalia slide out from under his arms and makes his way to the pool of water. Bearing his weight on his good knee, he crawls, his arms weak under his chest.

Bending his face to the pool, he cups it in his hands. He sips, knowing the effect it would have if he took in too much too soon. Repeating the process more times than he can count, he rests his back against the stone at his rear.

Courage helps him light the fire again. Courage to think about how long he has before starvation overtakes him, courage to consider what he needs to leave for Natalia when she wakes. Aside from the flint, he is not sure what he can truly do for her. He feels the water as it heals the agony in his mouth, the cooling effect it holds as it slides down the length of his burning throat.

Crawling back to her side, some color has seeped into her cheeks and a flush of red is on her lips. He brushes his hands through her hair, pulling his palm down to rest on the flesh of her neck. He finds her pulse stronger, but not strong enough to pull her back into consciousness.

His knuckles brush the side of her cheek. Astonished by her softness, he lets his fingers rest there, vibrant in the touch of her skin.

His heart thumping, his pulse racing, he leans inches from her lips. He stops and closes his eyes. He never should have waited so long. He soaks in her breath and lets her share his. He should have done so the very first moment they met, and he is grateful the stars dropped such a girl into his life.

His lips caress hers. Soft. Fierce. Moisture captures his lips as another tear sheds his eye. His eyes closed, he pulls away but holds onto the memory of her taste.

"I dreamt this was how we met," she whispers.

He half laughs, half sobs as he pulls her in for an embrace. Her head nestles in the nape of his neck. "I thought you were dead. I thought you were going to die."

"If I were to die, I think it would have happened long ago."

His arms remain wrapped around her tiny body. The smell of eucalyptus envelopes him. Resting his forehead against hers, he takes her in, the softness of her skin, the beat of her heart, the silk of her hair, even the velvet in her voice.

"How long have I been asleep?" she whispers.

"I'm not exactly sure," he says. "I was out for a while myself."

They hold each other in silence and allow the rise and fall of their chests to become one as they listen to each other's breathing.

"What's the bad news, Quinn?"

His forehead pulls back from her, his eyes twinkling. "How do you know there is bad news?"

Her hand runs down the length of his face. "Well, your face is wet."

"I fell in some water."

"Liar."

The color returns to her face as he gazes at her.

She returns the gaze and presses her hand against his chest. "Kiss me again."

He doesn't hesitate as his lips find hers. Pressing his body against hers, he parts his lips. Her actions mimic his. Gentle yet urgent.

His hand holds the back of her neck. Feeling her intake of breath, he finds the tender moisture of her lips and gives into his desires. His hands wrap into the strands of her hair as her hands find their way up the length of his shirt. His skin on fire, his breath shaking, his lips find the base of her neck. The moan that erupts from her mouth weakens his muscles, and his lips find hers once more.

Out of breath, and his lips tender with lust, he pulls away to stare into her face. She looks back at him with as much desire and affection as he could have hoped for.

They stare at each other in silence until at last the darkness of the cave reminds him of their plight. He whispers against her ear, "The volcano erupted. I don't know how many survived. And we are trapped in a cave."

She considers their surroundings, the smooth stone walls, the pool of water in the corner, the makeshift fire inches from them. And a door made out of boulders and unmovable stone. "I'm going to be honest, Quinn. I've seen better accommodations than this."

"Maybe we will have more luck opening the entrance with two of us."

"Because I am so strong? You're more delusional than you're letting on."

Standing up, he ignores his aching muscles and holds out his hand. She takes it without question and together they work at the boulders blocking the cave's entrance. They push instead of pull. They even try anchors from the sticks and rubble at their feet.

Their backs against the wall, sweat building on their skin, they stare at the stones with only the crackle of the fire to light the rocks.

He opens his arms to her, and she curls in like a bird finding a nest. Her head on his shoulders, her breathing rhythmic with his, they listen to the fire and watch the motionless stone entrance.

"Maybe another quake will hit and loosen them up," she whispers.

"Maybe."

"Or we find the source of the water. The foundation could be weaker there."

"It could."

"Find which crack in the rocks the fire's smoke is using to escape. Use the hole as our leverage."

"That could work."

They consider their options in stillness and accept the possibilities for what they are, and the optimism they stand for. They hold onto their illusions of success.

Silence wraps around them, and they both fall asleep.

Chapter Fifty-Two
Natalia

Quinn is weaker than he is letting on. My worry increases when he admits he slept for an unknown length of time. I can't ignore the signs of hunger, his so much more than my own. His muscles scream in their labored movements. His eyes, yellowing slightly, stay closed for longer and longer periods of time.

And he is feverish.

Blood stains his pants around his knee. While he sleeps, I gently pull at the ripped jeans to inspect the injury. His knee, swollen and caked in blood, has a gash thicker than that of my smallest finger. I soak one of my bandages in water and clean the wound, then wrap the cloth around his knee like a brace to shield the wound from infection.

The stone of the cave walls has become my solitude. They are my protection. My refuge. In my mind, the water outside has turned to black. The sun has turned to smoke. The jungle has become covered in solid rock. In my mind, the volcano destroyed everything.

I hold myself within these walls, sustaining life with each of my breaths. I hold onto each beat of my heart, holding onto the desire to fight for this life. Fight for his life.

Quinn now sleeps more often than he wakes. With life and its course through time, it is I who have become Quinn's Keeper. I feel like we have been here for days. Often, when he sleeps, I find loneliness. Other times, I find my recluse easier than any other alternative. It is the hope for others that allows death to come faster. To creep up to my soul and whisper comforts and love.

I keep my hope alive for Quinn. My hope for the hundreds of people I left trapped in a mountain of fire.

And I wait. I wait for Quinn to wake. I wait with my memories, held with no tears. I let the dark consume me, and I listen to the howls of the wind seeping in from outside. My heart beats endlessly over and over again.

Every moment of the day I find myself getting get hungrier and hungrier. I never faced this with my own Keeper. His magic kept me fed and nourished. But I can do no such thing for Quinn.

I stare at him for several minutes before I find enough courage to check his pulse. But I don't move away once I find it. I stay still and fearful of the air surrounding us like bubbles in a tub. I also check his knee. It looks frightfully painful, like a war wound just now setting in before he is about to crumple on the battlefield.

Isolation twists inside the normal comforts of my confines and pushes its way into my chest. It builds a hole in my ribs and pulsates through my veins. There are times when keeping the pressure inside is too hard. Too painful. So, when the tears drop freely, I let them fall one by one. I don't want to be doing this again. I don't want this for Quinn.

I think it is the silence that is slowly driving me mad. Silence that is so still it begins to vibrate in the air like mosquitoes. I try to hum and drown out the noise.

My bones aches and my muscles are stiff. There is a kink in my neck that makes me moan as I attempt to move.

I check my own wounds, nearly healed and invisible. Could the blue in my veins help save him? But in the dim light, I can't see a shimmer. Not enough to help hold him over while I build back my own strength.

If only he had his strength. If only I had more of my own.

I can't remember trying to escape my first cave of darkness. I remember begging for my freedom, screaming threats and making bargains that held no truth, but I do not remember an actual escape attempt.

Not until Quinn fell from the sky. It feels like a lifetime ago.

My eyes dart up at the memory. Seeing nothing but darkness, I pull a stick from the fire, a torch holding strong and bright in my hand. I toss it back and forth in between my hands, helping dissolve the heat from the fire.

I stretch my arm as high up to the ceiling as I can manage. My muscles strain as I tiptoe around the circumference of the cave. Gleaming white mushrooms hang in one corner like a chandelier. I brace my boots into the crevasses in the walls using as much leverage as possible. I use my legs to push up, and brace to grasp a handful of the fungi.

I drop down and crawl over to Quinn. He doesn't wake at my first attempt. Nor my second. I check his pulse, and drop what is left of my skirt into the pool of water to moistens his lips. When his eyes begin to stir, I urge him to drink more water.

"Slowly, now." My arms slip under his shoulders. "I need you to sit up, Quinn. Help me sit you up."

He obliges without question, his eyes sharp even in his weakened state.

"I need you to eat these. They are going to help." One by one I place the stems into his mouth.

He covers his mouth as he gags.

"Slowly now. Too much at once will make you sick."

With his hand still covering his lips, his eyes bulge at me. "Their taste is going to make me sick. What they hell are these?"

"They're mushrooms."

"They're disgusting! What did they grow from? Decomposing mold?"

I shrug my shoulders, unsure how to deny his claim. "They are going to keep you alive."

He grimaces but swallows the vile tasting fungi, then crawls to the pool of water. After several sips, he reaches his hand toward her. "All right, princess. I'll trust you."

"Queen."

His smile finds its way to me in the dim light. "Queen of Estancia."

I hand him two more mushrooms. He takes them from me without argument. He grimaces as he swallows the fungi down with more water.

"When I met you, you were barely a girl of any words." He bends into a crouch at the water, sweat pouring off his skin. "Now you insist you are my queen."

"No, Quinn. Not your queen. Just a queen of a land long lost and forgotten."

He crawls over to me and wraps his hands around her neck. "You've always been my queen."

His forehead touches that of my own. I am not sure how long we sit in each other's shadows. Even as his legs start to tremble and he shifts all his weight onto his good knees, he refuses to move. But I feel the quake in his chest and the tremble in his breathing.

"My dad is dead," he whispers.

My eyes pool with water as I think of Bailey. As I think of Quinn. I have no words for him, no reassurances that everything will be okay. No pleasantries about how life always finds away.

"Sing to me, Natalia," he says.

My own breath shakes as I think of words to help soothe him. I think of the songs of my past and the beat of my own father's heart. His, too, has ceased beating. Much longer ago of course. But even then, a father's trust in their child is all one truly needs to keep moving forward.

Lifelong hunt is far and wide,
Sacrifice, no longer at her side.
Born again, save my king,
Take my breath, hear me sing.

Rejoice in loss, blood drips cold,
Till the dragon, her bounty sold.
He took it all, fire and life,
Her heart lay pierced without the knife.

Be here not made, be here strong.
Grow from the ground, above it all.
You shall not falter; you shall not wither.
Shell of the winter, summer, and fall.
Be here not made, be here strong.

You will grow, you will stand.
Dragon breath, fire and ice.
Roots of gilt, fruits of silver.
Be here not made, be here strong.

His lips find my once more. His embrace fills the void of despair for us both, and my trials and worries no longer linger on my mind.

Chapter Fifty-Three
Quinn

Dust falls from the rocks at the top of the cave. It tickles his eyelashes and stick to his dry mouth. A thick layer of dirt covers his face. Caked there, like frost.

Natalia wakes and looks at the disturbance on the ceiling. "Do you think it's another quake?" she whispers.

"No. I think a quake would a little more violent."

"Animals?"

He tilts his head to ponder the idea and listens. Past the drips of water, and through the small rocks falling from the ceiling, he hears something so magnificent he rises to his feet though his thighs tremble with the forceful motion.

"Listen," he says.

He hears the faint beating of wings and familiar growls. He hears talons walking above their refuge.

"The dragon came for you."

She wrinkles her brow. "How?" She stands at Quinn's side.

"He was the one who brought us here. Showed me the way."

They hear murmurings outside. Rushed, panicked voices giving orders and the strenuous sounds of men moving rocks. As light cascades through the fissures, Quinn turns to Natalia and smiles.

His eyes dim through the small movement, and his hands tremble. She holds him by the waist, smiles, and nods her head.

Ryan stands at the base of the cave's entrance with smile plastered across his face so wide and full of cockiness, Quinn can't help but laugh.

Natalia lunges for him. He embraces her and lifts her feet off the floor. Her arms wrap around his neck, like lost siblings reuniting after disaster strikes.

Quinn falls as Natalia lets go. Catching himself on the stone to his side, he watches as Cyprien takes an apprehensive step into the cave's entrance. They nod at each other as Quinn stumbles into the sunlight.

Darius approaches Natalia at Ryan's side. The grief plastered across his face diminishes the second Natalia takes ahold of him, her arms circling around his waist. She cries into his shoulders. "I'm sorry, Darius. I am so sorry."

"Shush now." He takes a step back and holds her chin in between the palms of his hand. "I am fine. You saved me even after I abandoned you. It is me who needs to beg for your forgiveness."

"Let's beg for more forgiveness later," Ryan says. "It's time to get these two home."

Chapter Fifty-Four
Natalia

Two dragons circle overhead. One hovers closer than the other, with more blues than grays. The other hides the nakedness of its skin with wrinkles and lean muscle. Landing on the side of the mountain, their talons dig into the cliffs at the side of the vegetation.

My memories of the one are so strong, I hear the rise and fall of its chest in my sleep. The dragon looks upon me with a crystal-like glow in its eyes. When I first woke, I feared I had dreamed the dragon, but as he treks along the trail in front of me, I see the glistening magic dust off the scales on his tail. How could I ever not love such an amazing beast?

"They led us to you, Natalia. They sought us out and led us straight to you."

Cyprien's exhaustion is clear. The blue strings of his hair fall into his face. His pants are ripped at the knees. The sleeves of his tunic are frayed and covered in dirt.

He turns his head to Quinn, standing just outside the cave's entrance, timid, as if he has nowhere else to go. "Come, let us get you out of here. There is something you both need to see."

Although my strength has returned, Quinn's definitely has not. Relying heavily on Ryan and Darius to help him walk, he barely stays on his feet. My concern for him blots out any curiosity about what I need to see. "He can't make it, Ryan. He needs medicine. He needs to be fed."

He turns his attention to Quinn. "Dude, let us carry you," Ryan says quietly.

Quinn's voice cracks, but he shakes his head even as he stumbles. "Dude, no."

Ryan catches him as he falls. "I won't let Natalia see. I promise."

"Dude, no." He lets go of Ryan's shoulders and sits on the boulder at his feet. "I just need a minute."

"I don't have anything to give you here. A few miles down. Nothing more. Once we reach the bottom of the climb, I can fix this for you." He kneels closer to Quinn's face. "We can fix this."

Cyprien is watching with concern. "When was the last time he ate?" he asks.

"A few mushrooms. Nothing more. Days. Several days. But I think the wound on his knee is poisoning him. I think that is causing the true harm."

Ryan pulls up the pant leg on Quinn. The bandage has bleed through. He keeps at Quinn. "A few hours. I can get you there in just a few hours."

"I can walk." Quinn pulls himself to a stand, but immediately falls backward.

Darius catches him before his head hits the ground.

"Quinn, you can't walk. You can hardly stand." Ryan's tone is patient, filled with worry.

"I can't be carried either. I'd rather crawl."

Although ridiculously filled with pride, I understand his resolve. When life is at its lowest, when death and turmoil have outweighed every decision at your feet, resolve is often the only tangible aspect of life that holds weight.

Even if he is carried, I am sure he is miles away from any camp. I should have tried to close the wound. I should have gotten more mushrooms for him. I should have done so much more to try and help him.

Hearing the dragons flap their wings, my senses reach up to them. For as far as they have come, I refuse to let his trials end here. I remember the look in his eyes when I drew for him in our first camp. The way he looked into my eyes, past the desperation, past my fear or confusion. He swayed on his feet to my songs at the dragon carvings. I desperately wanted him to kiss me that night and desperately want more to come. For as far as Quinn brought me, I won't leave this mountain without him.

His eyes close and he loses consciousness. Ryan taps on his cheeks to wake him. Even Cyprien remains motionless at their side, with nothing left to say. My heart stops. In the face of death once more, my heart continues to break harder and harder.

Ryan turns to Darius. "Maybe if we take turns. Maybe we can get him down in shifts."

"Maybe If I run down, get help, bring it back here to him."

I turn me back on them. He needs more, and he needs more time. He needs his motivation. His determination. His hard will and stubbornness need to soar back to life. He needs his health. Strong and fierce. I begin to climb.

"Natalia, where are you going?" Darius says.

I ignore their calls. My boots crumble the rocks from my forceful strides. I lumber back up the trail they descended and climbs up the stones that kept me in yet another dungeon. Fumbling with hand grips, my boots find holds before my resolve fails. My feet slip on the rocks, but never stops. I climb until her fingers are raw.

I climb up the cliff vertical the empty cave Quinn and I survived through. I climb past the forest of my childhood. Past the tress Quinn found safety in as his father was murdered beneath him. I climb past my childhood hope to save an entire race of people. I climb with the hope to save one. Just one.

The men are screaming at me to come back, but I continue to climb until at last I reach the top. I stand at the top of the cliff, the ledge inches from my demise, and I search the skies. I search for the dragons. One in particular.

"Keeper!" My screams reach the heavens; for that I am sure. "Keeper!" I wait for the dragon, the all-knowing resolve held within me.

It appears once more just above the horizon. His partner steady at his side, they soar with the wind on top of the trees. They race over the never-ending greenery of a land I call my home. All of it, with all its mistakes. All the wrongs and misgivings. Because I also call it home through the prospects of hope. Of family. Of love. Both now and then. All of it is all an anomaly, because time is always with us. It is always there to give us hope.

The dragon's soaring slows as it approaches my calls. My focus and energy renew. "Keeper!"

Both dragons find landings on the cliffs at my side. Their bodies encircle each other, their scales arranged upon each other in perfect parallels. They are anxious at my words. Their faces are firm and still as they wait for my demands. They wait for my request.

"He is there,ason I am here Keeper, and he is dying." Tears fall down my face as I drop to my knees. "Please, please, help him."

Chapter Fifty-Five
Quinn

He wakes up in his bed at the villa. His sheets are pulled to his chin. His head rests on the fluff of his pillow. His mouth tastes of dust.

Wiggling his toes first, then his fingers. He tenses the muscles in his legs and arms. He exhales deep into his chest. His limbs feel good, and his mind is clear. He sits up. His bed coverings remain soft and warm to the touch. Natalia, with her arm under her head, rests at his side.

"Hello, Mr. Quinn," she murmurs.

"Hello, Ms. Natalia."

She mimics his posture and eyes him as he stretches and takes in the world around him.

"How are you feeling?"

"My body feels more alive than I have ever felt. Ever." His hands move to cover his face. His chest tightens as he holds back his emotions while his hands tremble and shake. Clasping them in his lap he tries to shield it from her, to be there for her, to be what she needs after such a draining ordeal.

His body is no longer fatigued or sore, nor is there any pain in his knee. But he feels life has drained from him. An emptiness holds in his gut that pulls at his heart. It pulls at his effort to appreciate the feel of his healed body. So much life has been taken. Santino. Gaeetan. Pops. People died he didn't even know, and the thought of the losses aches his heart.

He doesn't want her to see him so weak and fragile. But he also knows he lives because of her. He wills himself to pull it together while cradling the glass shards in his heart.

Chapter Fifty-Six
Natalia

His eyes hold grief. I can see it pull on him. The rise and fall of his chest quivers as he pretends to ignore it.

I, too, struggled with such moments when I woke in the cave. When hope was outweighed by sorrow. When refusing that sorrow became so heavy, the weight of it bore down so hard. "I want you to come downstairs with me."

"No. Not yet."

His hands wipe his worn face, and he swings his feet to the side of his bed. His back shields his emotions from my view. I crawl over to him and wrap my arms around his chest. His head drops into me, and my heart sinks. I know precisely what holds his thoughts.

"I will be right back, okay?"

He nods at me but does not speak.

Dark clouds cover his heart and there is only one thing that can sooth the storm brewing inside him. I know he needs to be alone right now. Wants to be alone right now. But I also know better. I let go and hurry to the door while he stares out the window.

Chapter Fifty-Seven
Quinn

When he was little and on one of his first excavations with his father, he came across a skull in the fields of Kyan. At first, he had been scared, fearful a haunted spirit would be angry at him for upsetting its resting place.

But as the skull was cleaned, polished, and examined, his father explained that history cannot be savored without such artifacts. Even that of a skull. Without the proof of life, there cannot be history. Everything Bailey ever found always had a story attached. A pot used to feed some children, a carving that marked the prayer for a loved one, and a skull that told the world how he ate, how he battled, and how he died.

Quinn was not ready to die, to let his body tell the history of his sorrow, of a life he had not yet started to live. He was not ready for history to take him. For death to take him. Yet, that is the only thing that holds his mind. Death. So much death.

His father was gone from him too soon. Taken. Ripped from the earth before he even had a chance to say a proper goodbye. He replays the moment over and over in his head. And no matter what he does, he can't seem to make it stop.

"I've decided you need to go to school."

He turns his head and his vision clouds. For a moment, he thinks he forced a change upon his memories. Wished it into being. But the cocky man in front of him is so much more than a memory.

He springs to his feet, rounds the bedframe, and grasps his father as they fall into each other. Their foreheads rest upon each other, their hands clasped around the other's neck.

His beating heart calms. "I thought you were dead."

"I think I might have been. Yes, I think I might have been."

Chapter Fifty-Eight
Natalia

Several days pass quietly in the villa as Quinn and Bailey recover from their injuries. Death brought them closer, and they have embraced it tighter than I could ever have imagined. They find ways to stay near and talk together. They laugh together. They go on walks together.

Although his glances at me remain heated and filled with temptation, I allow him his time. I allow both of them their time.

Cyprien sleeps on the couch with a sheet and pillow so different from what he would have known in Gaeetan's castle. But he doesn't seem to mind. He laughs with the others, helps clean up after meals, and forms a bond with Darius that seems to fulfil both their needs for friendship. It is a friendship based on awkward conversations, backwards puns, and total undisposed trust.

As I watch their dubious relationship blossom, I learn that once Ryan got Bailey to a safe location, he went back to the mountain. An absurdity really, but also not surprising. He found Cyprien and Darius struggling to save dozens of men and stepped in without question.

The entire mountain was destroyed without one single man inside. All except Gaeetan that is. A five-mile radius was obliterated. And in such trials as they experienced, Cyprien became a new member of Bailey's inner circle, carting more wine than beer into the villa and ironing his clothes for a lazy afternoon with simple camaraderie.

"Did you grow up with any money?" Cyprien says to Darius over a game of cards.

"Well, we had some. I mean I was fed and clothed," Darius says.

"So you were poor?"

"No. Not poor. Just on a budget…always."

"To me that sounds like you were poor." He plays a hand and Darius eyes him in playful annoyance.

"Was it hard?"

Darius tosses down a card. "No. I mean it was all I knew. Just different from growing up in a castle, I suppose."

"Are you still poor? Do you want some money?"

"No, I don't want some money."

"It sounds like you want some money."

"No, I don't want any money."

"I want some money," Ryan adds in.

Cyprien turns to look at Ryan. "How much? Because I am talking a lot more than just to settle a tight budget."

"Like enough money for a castle?" Ryan says.

"Wait. No. What?" Darius's eyes flash to Cyprien, his eyelids squinting, and his brow scrunches.

"I have a lot. Of money, I mean. And if you just supposed that I gave you some, what would you guys do with it?"

Ryan folds his hand on the table. His eyes find their way to me, quietly watching from across the room. "I would buy Estancia."

My gaze flashes to him, softening at his stare.

"Done."

Cyprien, too, looks to me. "But you need to figure out how to do it. My privileged life has left me extremely incompetent when it comes to working with the government."

Ryan picks up Darius's hand. "Do you have enough to build?"

"Why? Did you change your mind on the castle?" Cyprien says.

"Yes."

"No moats. But I suppose I could support a small castle."

I stand and edge closer to all three of them. "Why?"

Putting down his hand, Cyprien picks up the glass of wine at his side and leans back in his chair. "Because my family wronged you. I wronged you."

"You have never been anything but kind to me, Cyprien," I whisper, but halt mid-sentence.

He rocks on his chair. "Oh, but I did. I asked for something that you could not give. And truly, Natalia, I wish nothing more than your forgiveness."

"Cyprien, I hold no grudges against you."

Quinn enters the room, his weak knee supported with a cane in his hand. He sits at my side and takes my hand.

"Quinn, do you know how to build a castle?" Ryan says.

"What? No. Well, on video games maybe."

"Do you know how to buy land in Argentina?" Cyprien says.

"No, but I guess Pops does. I mean he bought this place, didn't he?"

Cyprien, Darius, and Ryan turn to each other smiling and make a toast. Wine to beer. Man to man to man.

"You don't need to do this," I whisper to Cyprien.

"Yes, yes I do."

Quinn takes Ryan's hand and makes the next play. "Do what? What are we doing?"

"We're building the Queen of Estancia a castle," Ryan says.

Quinn's eyes pop open. "Sweet. When do we start?"

Chapter Fifty-Nine
Quinn

She enters his room with her hair dropping over her face, her posture hesitant. Dressed in green linen with a small wooden chestnut hanging around her neck, the smell of eucalyptus fills the room. The dress she wears mimics the one from the stream the first time they met. It hangs off her shoulders, enticing him to get a closer look.

Sitting at the edge of his bed, she unlaces her boots and one by one, places them next to his at the foot of his bed. Her golden slippers nowhere to be found.

She lies on the top of his covers with flushed cheeks. Her fingertips cross the bedding to brush through his hair. She is uncertain. "I don't know how to do this," she whispers.

He embraces her as he lies down at her side and his mouth finds comfort in hers. Temptation rages through him as she arches her back, the lust clear with the touch of her skin. She gasps as his fingers move up the length of her sides.

She runs her fingers underneath his shirt and pulls it above his head. Her palms make their way back down to his abdomen, forcing his breath to quicken. His fingers race up to the nape of her neck, and move her hair out of his way. His lips crash into the side of her neck and relish the sweetness of her skin.

Yet he pulls back, lust overtaken with emotion. "I don't know how to do this either," he confesses.

With red blushing onto her cheeks, she giggles softly. "I love you, Quinn."

"I love you, Natalia." He brushes his lips across her forehead and settles at her side. He pushes more fallen strands of hair out of her face as he takes her in. Her olive skin, her raven eyes, her blood red lips. All are nothing compared to her heart of gold. The true treasure that lies within.

Chapter Sixty
Natalia

We arrive at Estancia with packs on our backs and hope in our hearts. Hope of a future for all of us. But when we pass the grove of chestnut trees, it is not just me who becomes breathless. They all stop and drop their packs. Quinn and Bailey. Ryan and Darius. Even Cyprien.

The ground is covered in tents, huts of grass, and homes of clay. Hundreds stand still at their approach. I glide through the camp, my eyes searching for a reason.

One by one, the people I pass drop to their knees. The men, women, and children of Kinoda. The farmers and merchants of Iritan. Even Gaeetan's dirty old guards. Horace's height nearly matches mine even on his knees.

Their fists clench at their hearts.

Two dragons circle overhead, then land in the fields to the west. They, too, drop their heads to the ground.

Silence overtakes the noise of hundreds.

Turning to my companions, my face fills with dismay and my cheeks flush. Cyprien falls to his knees first. Bowing to me, as his very own title falls at his feet in front of me. Ryan, Darius, and Bailey follow suit next, their eyes tearful with pride.

Quinn approaches cautiously, just close enough to allow me to hear his whispers as he drops to one knee, a smile spread across his face like the stars. "Like I said, Ms. Natalia, you have always been my queen."

I was groomed as an heir to the throne. Destined to be the Queen of Estancia, in a noble house filled with my own personal court and guards ordained to protect me at all costs.

My father had seen a chestnut blossoming from the ruins. A girl who mattered so much more alive than sacrificed to a crown. This is the purpose of my sacrifices. The true prophecy of my life. These people. Each and every one of them. *They* are my purpose.

The true treasures of Estancia, my family, kneel at my side.